# BIG 3

## A REVERSE HAREM ROMANCE

STEPHANIE BROTHER

This book is a work of fiction. Any resemblance to persons, living or dead, or places, events or locations is purely coincidental. The characters are all productions of the author's imagination.

Please note that this work is intended only for adults over the age of 18 and all characters represented as 18 or over.

ISBN: 9798683709075

# CONTENTS

# 1

I'm not sure what is worse: finding out that Nate is a cheater or having to pack to leave him while he watches. There's so much shame in discovering that the pathetic feelings I had were all just an illusion, and even more shame in realizing that the man I thought I loved is an asshole.

"Why are you so dramatic about this? Did you seriously think that we were exclusive?" Nate's face curves into a sly smile that sets the hairs on my arms raising. Oh God. Why didn't I see this side of him before my heart got involved? Why didn't I realize that he was deceitful and cruel? He charmed and flattered me into this relationship for what? So he could stick his dick into anything that moved while pretending to be the perfect boyfriend. I don't even know what else to say.

"You called me your girlfriend." My voice is high pitched and raised, which only makes him smile more.

"Well, you are, Natalie," Nate says slowly as though he thinks I'm too stupid to grasp words spoken at a normal rate. "The other girls…well, they're just there for the physical side. To do the things you won't do."

I grit my teeth as I toss the last of my clothes into the suitcase. Nate's eyes follow me from where he's lounging against the doorjamb. Of course, this is all my fault. Just because I wouldn't let him stick his dick in my ass, is that seriously how he's going to justify his constant infidelity? I've given this man a year of my life. My photographs have turned his travel blog from third-rate to go-to. I'm what's catapulted his income from subsistence hostel level to five-star. And this is what I get for my efforts? He hasn't paid me for any of it.

I guess he'd say that I've had the experience of a lifetime. He's supported all my living expenses for the entire time we've been traveling, but now I've seen what a lowlife he is, I'm walking away with nothing. Worse than that, I've had to call Mom to book me a flight home.

There are a million things that I could tell him right now, but I don't have it in me to try and argue with a man who will never accept he's in the wrong.

"You can't expect me to be satisfied with just this." He waves his hand across the room, as though our life together has been so boring to him. "We're not married. This is the time for us to experience everything we can before we settle down together."

"Settle down. You seriously think that I'd want to settle down with you, knowing what you've done." Of course, Nate didn't share our open-relationship status with me. I had to find it out from a well-meaning waitress who'd seen Nate with three women in the past week. I'd been telling her all about what an amazing boyfriend he was for buying me a silly necklace, and she took pity on me. She'd gone through something similar herself and couldn't stand to see another rat-bastard (her words) get away with it. Thank goodness. This charade could have gone on and on. Would he ever have been honest?

No. I know that for sure.

His lies gave him something to hold over me. I was loyal to him, and he wouldn't have wanted it any other way. As if he would have accepted me fucking other men. I think about the men I've met on our travels, back to Marley and his smooth brown skin and amazing physique. He'd liked me. I'm pretty certain of that. We could have had amazing sex. He had hands big enough to crush Nate's stupid head like a nut. Hands big enough to hold me while he fucked me against one of the palm trees on the beach in Jamaica. Or Marco. That man had liquid chocolate eyes and a smooth Italian accent that could slide the panties from even the most uptight of women. He was a charmer for sure, but I bet he would have been passionate between the sheets.

So many men. So many missed opportunities.

And how would Nate have compared? There's no way he would ever have accepted me discovering that his dick was smaller or his body less toned. Orgasms have been few and far between recently, as though he's given up caring about my pleasure. He's become lazy as his cheating has increased.

Well, fuck him. Fuck all men who think they can have their cake and eat it too.

"I have the ring," he says. "It's in the nightstand. Take a look."

"What?"

"The ring," he says again slowly, and I want to punch him in the face. I'm not looking anywhere except in the bathroom for my make-up bag. I'm out of here. He can give his lying, cheating ring to one of his other women –

the one who took it up the ass like the trooper that I'm definitely not.

"I don't want to look at a ring," I reply equally slowly. "My cab will be here in five minutes."

"Natalie." He shakes his head like a teacher who has caught a pupil eating candy in class. "Always the drama queen. Are you really going to go through with this? You know we have flights to Cambodia in two days. Just think about Angkor Wat and the spectacular shots you'll be able to take there. It's the chance of a lifetime."

"There'll be other chances," I say, but even as the words pass my lips, I don't believe them. I know what I'm walking away from, and it's killing me. Tomorrow I'll be home with my tail between my legs, an empty bank account, and no job. Traveling around the world is going to be the last thing on my mind. This morning I was sitting on the balcony staring out at the swelling sea, filled with false hope. By tomorrow, I'll be back home to an uncertain future.

"Why give up this one?" He saunters into the room as though we're discussing which of the five hotel restaurants to eat in this evening, rather than the acrimonious end of our lives together. "I didn't know this is how you'd react. If I'd known…"

"You'd what?"

"I'd have talked to you…explained how important it is to me that we experience all aspects of pleasure together. If you'd accepted that…"

I put up my hand because I just don't want to hear any more bullshit. As though the universe is listening with my same disgust, the phone rings. It's Connie, and I couldn't be more relieved to see a friendly name pop across the screen.

"Hey, Connie," I say, turning my back on Nate and heading to the bathroom.

"Natalie. I got your message. Are you seriously coming home tonight?"

"Seriously," I say, kicking the door closed and holding the phone against my ear with a raised shoulder while I gather my toiletries.

"That's amazing. I can't wait to see you."

"Me too. It's been too long." It really has been. A year without my bestie has been tough. Yes, technology makes the world smaller, but video chats aren't the same as sitting on the same sofa and sharing a bottle of wine. I've missed my friend, and now that my heart is shredded, her warm words and kindness feel even more distant.

"I know your mom moved last September. How do you feel about moving in?"

"Okay, I guess. She's pretty much ordered me to live with her. There are about ten spare rooms for me to choose from, and the house is right on the beach."

"That'll be perfect. You can sun yourself while you get used to being on home ground."

"No rest for me," I say. "I'll need to find work straight away."

"I'm sure something will come up, and in the meantime, let your rich stepfather put his hand in his pocket." Connie chuckles evilly. Conrad Banbury is richer than Croesus. The house I'm going to be staying at temporarily is just one of many, and worth well over fifteen million big ones. I guess he can afford to keep me for a while, but it's not something I'd feel comfortable with at all. I mean, I've only met the man once before I left the U.S. with Nate, and that was a rushed brunch where Mom laughed nervously and fluttered her hands too much.

"Conrad has generously paid for my flight home. I think that's about all I'm okay with him doing."

"I should think so too. He probably found the money for the ticket down the back of his designer couch."

"Probably."

"So, let's meet for lunch on Wednesday. My treat."

"Sounds good. My diary is wide open." I blink quickly as tears spring to my eyes. The amazing itinerary that I'd planned out with Nate is now an unfulfilled dream. Once I'm back in the States, my passport will find its way back into a dusty drawer.

"We'll go to that taco place you love. And for ice-cream sundaes after, okay?" I can hear how desperately Connie is trying to make my return less painful.

"That sounds great." My response is only half honest.

We say our goodbyes, and I inhale deeply before I tug the door open. Nate is relaxing in one of the plush teal velvet bucket seats, one leg resting on the other knee like a bored celebrity. His eyes are fixed to his phone, so I ignore him and stuff my toiletry bag into my bulging case. Sweat pricks at my armpits and my upper lip despite the air-conditioning.

It takes so much force to close the case that I'm out of breath by the time I'm done. All I need to do now is check the room and my travel documents and get my purse packed for the journey. There's a hollow and shaky feeling in my chest and heat on my cheeks that is only partially related to how hot I am. Doing this with Nate's eyes on me is just the final humiliation.

"Natalie. Just sit down for a minute," he says, waving to the matching vacant chair next to him. "You look like you're struggling, and we should talk. This is all very hasty."

"I'm not going to sit down." I glance around the room, spotting my phone charger and my camera's charge pack on the ornate desk. Two things I'd be lost without. There's a bottle of water there too, and I snag it for my purse. By the time I'm done here, I'm going to need a quenching drink – something to wash away the bitter taste in my mouth. The room's phone starts to ring, and I know it's reception notifying me of the arrival of my airport transfer. Nate's expression darkens as he realizes this whole situation is about to come to an end. He's about to lose control. All of his pretense at calm is wiped away that second, and I get a glimpse of how he really feels. It isn't pretty.

After I've told reception I'll be down in a minute, I feel even more frantic. While Nate was all smooth words and relaxed gestures, I was okay. Now, something in my gut is telling me things could get ugly.

I toss the strap to my purse over my shoulder, grab my camera bag, and heft my suitcase onto the pristine white tiled floor. It makes such a loud thud that Nate's shoulders rise and his face contorts.

"NATALIE."

My heart accelerates, the pounding echoing through the emptiness behind my ribs. My feet propel me toward the door, not looking to see if Nate has stood from his chair. I fumble with the handle but manage to get it open and shove my case into the corridor. Two businessmen are walking past, and I'm grateful to fall behind them, hoping that Nate won't make a scene when he has an audience. At the elevators, I chance a look back at the room and see the man who's been my life for too long standing with his arms folded, watching me walk away.

How many hours did we spend together, hours that I will never get back? How can someone who was everything to me yesterday be nothing to me today?

As the elevator doors close, all the effort it took to hold myself together suddenly feels too much. My shoulders slump, and my chest hitches, squeezing a sob from my throat that elicits glances from the others standing around me.

Shit.

I can't make a scene. I don't want people's eyes on me, or their pity. It's just another layer of humiliation. Another deep breath forces down the swell of misery and disappointment.

I can do this. I can make it home.

And once I'm there, I'll have to force myself to move on because there really is no other way. Who knows what lays in store for me?

A blank page.

It's a scary thought. But I know one thing for sure. No man is ever going to have the chance to make a fool of me this way again. My shattered heart is getting put into a metal box and locked away. I won't be an idiot twice.

# 2

There's a pristinely uniformed limousine driver waiting for me in the airport with my name in ornate cursive. Natalie Monk. As soon as I read it, I remember how Nate used to snigger any time someone would call my name. Funny that I was never conscious of it before, but now it feels weird to see it written so boldly.

"Hi, that's me," I say, nodding at the sign.

The round-faced man smiles and puts the sign under his arm, reaching for my suitcase. "I'm Daryl. You get stuck in immigration?"

"I think it was just backed up."

I follow him out of the terminal building to a ridiculously long car, which is more luxurious than anything I've ever ridden in. As Daryl puts my luggage in the trunk, I slide into the cavernous interior, marveling at the soft leather seats and shiny walnut trim. There's even a section for drinks and glasses, and I get a craving for a gin and tonic even though I'm completely shattered from the journey. I just need something to take the edge off, but I stop myself, instead retrieving a perfectly chilled bottle of water.

I don't think Mom would approve if I show up smelling of alcohol at this time of the day. She's probably already disappointed about what's happened. She really liked Nate. He had a way of flattering her subtly that impressed her a lot. I haven't told her what he did yet. It's too humiliating. All she knows is that we've broken up, and that's all I'll be sharing.

The drive toward the coast is scenic, but I'm so tired that I let my eyelids close and rest my head against the side of the vehicle, my mind battling with all the things I didn't say to Nate. An hour passes before the driver slows, pressing a buzzer, which jolts me from my tortured rest, and informing whoever is on the other end of the intercom that I've arrived.

Large iron gates open automatically, and the car makes its way up a long driveway on an upward incline. I guess the house is perched up high. That'll make the views spectacular.

Mom told me that they have a private beach. Imagine. This isn't the life I grew up with. Dad worked in a bank, and mom was a personal assistant in a big corporation. We lived in an everyday house with a regular car. When Dad passed away, Mom kept us going with Dad's life insurance. Then she met Conrad just over a year ago and everything changed.

I feel like an imposter when the driver opens the door for me, and I'm left to walk to the double-height doorway with just my purse as a shield. I have no idea what to expect.

What I get is my mom appearing at the door before I can even ring the bell.

"Natalie." She pulls me into a perfumed hug that doesn't feel familiar. She smells expensive, and the silk kaftan she's wearing is nothing like I've ever seen her in before. She's turned into a Stepford wife in my absence and I don't like it. Mom was the only familiar thing I had to return to and now she's different.

"Hey, Mom."

She draws back, gripping me by the shoulders with her manicured fingers, scanning me with overly made-up eyes. "You look thin."

I glance down at myself, even though I know I'm wearing baggy pants and a loose blouse that doesn't reveal anything of my body shape. Nate liked it when he could feel my hip bones. He was always telling me how pretty they were, and I've been so busy. It's hard to find time to eat when you're constantly on the move.

"And you look tired."

Wow, she's full of compliments today.

"It was a long flight." I smile as broadly as I can force because I don't need an argument on the doorstep. Especially after yesterday's misery.

"Natalie." Conrad appears in the wide hallway, dressed exactly the way you'd expect of a semi-retired millionaire, with a broad sparkling grin that probably cost fifty thousand dollars in veneers. "It's so good to have you home."

Home. That's a generous statement, bearing in mind I've never crossed this threshold before. I guess I should be grateful for the generosity and just put away my prickliness. "Thanks," I say. "For the flight and for letting me stay. It won't be for long."

"Don't be silly." Mom waves her arm in an expansive movement. "This house is huge. It's no trouble at all.

Come. I'll show you to your room. I picked the best one with an ocean view to die for. I know how much you love the ocean. Really, it is the most spectacular place to live."

Conrad chuckles, putting his hands into the pockets of his tan slacks. "Your mom really loves it here." There's so much fondness in his expression that any doubts I had about his relationship with my mom fade a little. "I'll be in my office. Let me know what time dinner will be served."

Mom leads me up the glass-sided staircase, and we're followed by a man dressed in a shirt and formal black dress pants, who's appeared with my luggage. It's such an amazing home, with ridiculously high ceilings and softly colored chalky walls covered with expensive art. My sandals clap against the polished oak floors as we make our way down a long corridor. At the end, Mom opens a door to a room that exceeds the size and décor of any of the amazing hotels I've stayed in on my journeys, and that is saying something. But I'm not focused on the huge bed or the amazing silver crushed-velvet sofa for long. The room has bi-fold doors that open out onto a balcony overlooking the sea, and Mom is right. The view really is stunning.

"Wow," I say, dropping my purse on the bed and practically pressing my nose against the glass. Mom lifts the handle and slides the doors aside, and I'm caught in a breeze that smells of heaven. The shushing sound of the waves is like a balm to my tired mind. There is a small rattan sofa with light gray cushions on the balcony. I slump into it, unable to tear my eyes away from the turquoise of the ocean that spreads before me like an undulating blanket.

"It really is something special, isn't it," Mom says with a sigh. "You know, I wondered if I'd stop noticing the view after I'd been here for a few months, but I haven't. It still takes my breath away every day."

She takes a seat next to me and crosses her legs, resting her hands on her knees. "I'm glad you're home," she says. "I've been worried about you in all those places."

"I was always fine," I say. "But it's good to be back."

"So Nate is continuing on without you?" She's fishing for more information about what happened, but I don't blame her. I was very vague on the phone.

"Yes. He'll be in Cambodia tomorrow."

Mom screws up her nose but doesn't say anything. She's never been a traveler and doesn't have a concept of how vast and awe-inspiring the world really is. Countries that don't have the standards of development that she is used to aren't appealing to her in the slightest. "Well, I'm sure he's really going to miss you."

I know it's my fault that she's so in the dark about Nate, but her comment still stings. I imagine Nate convincing one of the other girls he's been fucking to join him on his trip. Maybe he'll buy her a camera and see if she can take some shots of the temples at Angkor. They won't be as good as mine would have been, but maybe he won't care as long as he can stick his dick where the sun doesn't shine.

"He'll be fine," I say, then decide to change the subject so that I don't get dragged into a debate. "I'm meeting up with Connie tomorrow. She's going to take me out for lunch."

"Well, that's just lovely. Something for you to do. Your stepbrothers won't be home for a couple of days, so you'll be stuck with Conrad and me for company."

"That's fine," I say. "It'll be good for us to catch up." Why she thinks I'm interested in the comings and goings of strangers, I've no idea. I wonder if she's forgotten that

I've never met Conrad's sons. I'm sure she told me their names at some point last year, but I can't recall.

"So, what would you like to do now? Maybe take a nap…get rid of those dark circles?"

"Yes," I say. "That would be amazing."

"Then I'll come and wake you for dinner. And maybe a walk along the beach. You really have to see it up close."

"Perfect."

Mom reaches out to squeeze my leg. "Welcome home," she says, and I smile even though I know I'm going to sob into the pillows on the elaborately carved bed as soon as she leaves. Home is where the heart is, and I think I've lost mine somewhere between here and Bangkok.

# 3

"You've lost weight," Connie says as she tugs me into a hug outside my favorite restaurant. "But we're going to fatten you up some today."

"I'm counting on it," I say, my stomach growling at the delicious smell of Mexican food wafting from Taco Loco. There were days, even when we were in Mexico itself, where I had cravings for the food from this place. I'm practically salivating.

We head inside and are immediately seated in a booth outside under the wooden pergola. The waitress hands us menus, and I glance over mine, even though I could recite it in my sleep. She places the complementary virgin strawberry daiquiris on the table with a bowl of chips and Connie recites our usual order. When the waitress has rushed off to request the mountain of food she noted in her pad, Connie reaches across the table to squeeze my hand.

"Nate's an asshole. Pure and simple. And you're better off without him."

"Broke and alone, you mean." I nibble a salty corn chip as my throat tightens.

"Single, sexy, and talented as hell is what you should be saying. He didn't deserve you. He was all hot air and no substance. You just couldn't see it."

Wow. Is that what Connie really thought of Nate? She never said anything negative about him to me in the past. "He lied to my face, and the worst thing is that I don't know how many times he was unfaithful. He wouldn't tell me. He just said that none of it mattered to him, and it shouldn't matter to me."

"Yeah, that sounds like something Nate would say. What a dick. Did he seriously think you were going to forget about it all?"

"Yes. He actually did. You know the worst part. He actually tried to blame me…because I wasn't up for some of the things he wanted to do in the bedroom."

"DICK," Connie hisses. "You're entitled to do what the hell you want in the bedroom. No one should ever feel under pressure to do anything they don't want to do. That's fucking abuse."

I look down at the table, tears pricking at my eyes as I tear away pieces of the paper napkin. I hear what Connie's saying, but there is still a part of me that wonders if I'm just too uptight. I mean, people are doing all sorts of kinky sex things these days. Look how mainstream BDSM has become after that book. I just didn't feel comfortable moving things in that direction with Nate, and I'm not sure if it was because of my own limitations or because I just never felt that his demands really involved my pleasure at all. It was all about him satisfying his own needs. That's not how sex should be.

"You've done the right thing," Connie says. "It can be really easy to be swayed when you're in a relationship. We all end up changing a little to fit with the people we love."

I nod because that is true. Look at Mom. She's transformed herself to fit in with Conrad's lifestyle, and she's so happy about it. I guess change doesn't always have to be a bad thing.

"I don't know what I'm going to do, Con. I've just been cruising around with Nate, imagining that one day everything that he was building with my help was going to be ours. I thought we were a partnership. I don't even have enough cash in my bank account to pay for this meal."

"Don't worry about that." Connie waves. "This is on me, and there's no point in looking back with regrets, honey. All experiences are there to learn from."

"Believe me, I've learned…the hard way."

"Anyway, it's time to look to the future," Connie says, tugging her big brown suede purse onto her knee and rummaging around inside. "I have something for you." She passes me a stack of folded papers.

"What's this?"

"Let's just say it's a happy coincidence."

I open the paper and read an address and information regarding a photo shoot taking place tomorrow. It's at a warehouse downtown. I look up, my brow furrowed, and find Connie beaming.

"You know I'm working as a PA right now. Well, the publisher is branching out into erotic romance. They need some shots to feature on a new trilogy. They have high hopes that it's going to hit the bestseller list. Anyway, the photographer is in the hospital with a burst appendix, and they need someone last minute."

"I don't do studio shots," I say, lowering the papers.

"But you can." Connie is practically vibrating with excitement. "The model… I've seen his portfolio. He's so hot."

"I'm sure he is, but it's not my area of expertise."

"It's paying good money. Look at the back."

I turn the papers over and find the payment schedule. A little puff of air escapes my lips. That's not money to turn down, but I don't know if I can do this. Raising my shoulders, I shake my head, and Connie's face falls. "I just don't know."

"You can do this," she says firmly. "And anyway, I don't have time to find anyone else."

I inhale deeply, thinking about the last shots I took of the sunsets in Thailand. It was worlds away from a muscly half-naked guy in a seductive pose, but there's no way I can let Connie down when she's put herself on the line for me. That, and I need the money badly.

She grins, taking a long sip of her pink drink that leaves sugar over her red-glossed lips. "It's going to be great. I know it…and if you need any help oiling up the models, you just let me know. I'll be happy to whizz across town to assist."

Connie's confidence in me is likely misplaced, but we'll find out one way or another tomorrow. This could be interesting or a disaster, but as Connie says, every experience can be learned from. I guess I'm going to be learning tomorrow!

# 4

Conrad insists that his driver drops me to the downtown warehouse where I'm going to be working. I don't argue because I'm still jetlagged and have no energy to work out where I'm going or how I'm going to get there.

As I step out of the limo, I don't miss the interested looks that turn disinterested as soon as they see me emerging in my baggy orange Thai-style pants and loose black linen blouse. There's no designer bags or celebrity outfits here, despite the luxury of the car. I hold tightly to the handle of my camera bag, tugging my large embroidered purse onto my shoulder as a gust of wind whips my short hair across my face. Gazing up at the huge warehouse building, I take a deep breath, designed to steady my nerves.

I spent much of yesterday afternoon browsing online for book covers, noting the poses and lighting used to bring out the best in the male models. I'm as prepared as I could possibly be with no direct experience and little notice, but that hasn't banished the fluttering butterflies from my belly. I couldn't even stomach breakfast, so I'm running on a double espresso. Maybe that's why I feel so wired.

It's now or never, I think, psyching myself up to push the door open.

The reception area is cavernous, and a single woman sits dressed in white at a clear glass desk with just a laptop and headset to work with. I approach slowly, gazing around at the polished concrete walls and floor.

"I'm Natalie Monk. I'm here for the shoot."

The woman nods and taps on her keyboard. "Take the elevator to the third floor. Andre will meet you and show you where to go."

The elevator is slick, moving faster than I'm expecting. Andre is at least six foot five, with pretty almond-shaped eyes and an outfit equally as white as that of reception lady. "Natalie," he croons. "So happy you could make it. We really didn't know what we were going to do when Alistair Cristie dropped out."

Alistair Cristie was the photographer they had lined up for this shoot? Shit. I am out of my depth. If the publisher is prepared to pay for someone that established for this shoot, they really are expecting this book to be a huge seller.

I follow Andre into a large space, which is set up like a hotel room. A king-sized bed with crisp white linen and enough pillows to cushion Satan's fall from the heavens stands next to a gorgeous ornate window. There's a desk and a plush sofa too. My mind starts to flick through all the possible shots I could get.

"You can set up here," Andre says, waving to a large table. Connie had assured me that they had much of the larger equipment that I would need, including lighting. I dump my bags on the table and begin to pull out my camera, flash, and lenses. I clean everything meticulously while Andre disappears through another door. A young girl who can't be much older than eighteen pushes a clothing rack into the room. There's a screen set up – I'm assuming for the model to change behind – and the costumes are set to the side.

"Can I get you anything," she asks. "Coffee? Breakfast muffin? Croissant?"

Whiskey, I think, but I don't verbalize it. I don't want her reporting back that I'm a morning drinker. But I'd kill for something that would burn on the way down and settle my nerves.

I start by taking some test shots, then adjust the position of the soft-box lighting. I want to get as much organized before I'm faced with an oiled-up muscle man.

A deep laugh rumbles through the door I came through. I'm assuming that it belongs to the model, but I don't turn. I keep my focus through my lens. My camera has always been a protection of sorts. It hides my face and masks my expression. Through it, I become a distant observer.

The rustle of clothes being removed is unmistakable. I know there are a number of shots to achieve today, involving a number of different outfits. We're due to start with the billionaire look, which I've learned involves a white shirt that has to be open at the neck to show plenty of tan skin, with and without a suit jacket and with and without a necktie. I chuckle, thinking about the reality of billionaires in the real world. Most are middle-aged geeks who struck rich in tech firms, or they're oil-rich or weapons rich. Not really the kind of men that any young woman in her right mind would be lusting over for anything other than money. Now in the book world, billionaires are something else entirely. Heavily muscled and below the age of thirty, it's a high-fantasy area of romance.

Now, I'm all for fantasy. My reality has proven to be far from satisfying, that's for sure. Today is all about bringing that fantasy to life for all the women out there who need to step out of their own existence for just a tiny moment. I understand that need completely.

The sound of someone clearing their throat interrupts my train of thought, and I jump, allowing my camera to drop from my face.

Oh.

My.

Goodness.

I swear I hear harps and violins and the flap of doves' wings. Angels swoon in the heavens at the sight of the man standing before me. All words slide out of my head and onto the polished gray floor between us. He slips his hands into the pockets of his impeccable black suit and cocks his head to the side, his blue eyes twinkling and dimples out in full force.

Oh Lord. That isn't fair. Blue eyes and dimples are a double shot of sexy, and I've never been able to keep my head when hot men are around.

I should have told Connie to find someone else. I knew that this was a disaster waiting to happen.

"Your mouth is open," the man says.

My lower jaw snaps upward like he ordered it into place, clinking my teeth in the process. I must look like a demented fish, but I can't seem to snap out of this mesmerized state.

"I'm Mason." He frowns now as though he's gone from being amused to being worried about my mental state.

Somehow, I get my brain to engage. "I'm Natalie."

"I know." That megawatt smile reveals perfect straight white teeth that could be featured in a toothpaste commercial. "The agency told me who was shooting today."

"That was organized of them."

"Makes a change."

We stand awkwardly for a few more seconds. Well, I'm the awkward one, and Mason looks totally at ease in his billionaire's suit, and as I gaze at him, I understand the fantasy one hundred percent. This man looks as though he could take care of every challenge that life could throw: big strong hands and muscles, a confident air, and a spark of humor. I actually pity the women who Mason turns his attentions to seducing. They wouldn't have a chance.

"So, where do you want me?"

There are many answers to that question that heat my cheeks. On top of me, beneath me, pressing my face into the pillow as he pounds me from behind. I don't know where that last one came from because that has never been my thing. Until now, it seems!

"By the desk," I say. "Let's start there."

After twenty minutes of shooting, I can confirm that Mason is a pro. He's at ease with the camera and fluid in his body. He knows the angles and expressions that will make a great shot, and he works it. I barely have to give him instruction.

I step back to the table, plugging my camera into my laptop so I can view the images, and Mason waits patiently.

"I think we've nailed that one," I say. "Let's move on to the next one."

"Sure." Mason strolls behind the screen, and I can't tear my eyes from him. The way he walks is so relaxed and sexy. He took his jacket off for the last few shots, and I can see his muscles working beneath the thinner fabric of his button-up shirt. When he disappears from view, I shake my head, trying to knock some sense into myself.

The next shots are Mason in jeans and a tight white tee. These shots are going to be more laid back, and Mason's body is going to be more revealed. I pull my water bottle from my purse and take a long cool drink, hoping to suppress the heat that's been developing since Mason walked into the room.

It works until he appears again, looking like a modern, rougher version of James Dean. I swear looking as good as Mason should be illegal. "Can you stand by the window?" I say, imagining the natural light casting across the white of his shirt and illuminating his eyes.

"Sure."

I move closer, my camera poised, pleased with how amazing the shot is. Mason turns to me, his expression about as panty-melting as I've ever seen it, and my heart skips. It's a pose, nothing more, but it's as though he's looking at me, wanting me. That's a serious skill he's developed.

"You've taken some amazing shots." He leans against the exposed brickwork, resting his hand on the window ledge.

"You're easy to photograph," I say, wondering how he knows what the images from today look like.

"The ones in Thailand are my favorite. The way you captured the sunrise over the monumental Buddha, that was something else."

I stop trying to find the best position to stand and straighten up, lowering my camera. "You've seen those?"

"Yeah…they made me want to see the place, for sure."

The ache in my chest that's been there since I discovered Nate's betrayal, but had dissipated a little since I was focused on Mason, returns. I loved Thailand. I loved all the places I visited. This downtown venue would never live up to the excitement of traveling, but I'm flattered that Mason likes my work.

"Well, that's what they're supposed to do," I say.

"Is that guy your boyfriend?" Mason folds his lips in to moisten them.

"No." The word comes out abruptly, revealing everything I didn't want Mason to know.

"You got a boyfriend?" His gorgeous lips quirk at the corner.

"Maybe I've got a girlfriend."

"Nah," he says. "Nothing wrong with that, of course. In fact, the idea is hot as hell, but I don't get that vibe from you."

I frown. "What vibe do you get?"

Mason shakes his head. "If you have lunch with me, I'll tell you."

"Who says we're breaking for lunch? We've got shots to get through."

He slides his hand into the pocket of the blue jeans that are hugging his ass and thighs just perfectly. "Nothing comes between me and food, Natalie. That's one thing you need to know about me."

At that moment, the girl who wheeled in the clothes appears holding a tray. "Ah, there you are," Mason says, striding forward.

"Sorry," she gasps, "the line was really long."

"Nothing to be sorry about," Mason croons. "Thank you."

She places the tray on the end of my table, and Mason flops onto a plastic chair, tearing off a chunk of one of the biggest muffins I've ever seen and tossing it into his mouth. "Mmmmm," he moans. "There really isn't anywhere else in the world that makes better muffins than Mama's Bakery."

"You want to break for a coffee and lunch? When are we going to get these shots finished?"

"We'll get them. Tell you what. If we work through, we can grab an early dinner. How about that?"

"That sounds completely unnecessary," I say. "We could both head home for dinner."

"And that sounds completely boring." Mason's eyes sparkle with a challenge. Being boring was something Nate used to toss at me whenever I wouldn't do what he wanted me to do. Fuck that. I'm not getting manipulated by another asshole.

"Well, I'm good with being boring."

Mason's eyes scan me as though he's trying to read what's going on in my head. He reaches to the tray and takes the spare muffin, holding it out to me. "You have to try this." It's an order but worded gently. More of a plea. My stomach growls, and Mason smiles. "You see…you really do need this muffin."

I reach out and take it from his hand, finding it's still warm. The first bite is tentative, but he's right. It's nectar from the gods. After that, I don't care that he's watching me stuff my face. I feel hunger like I haven't felt for months.

When I've finished, I find him smiling with a faraway look in his eyes that I just can't decipher.

Mason is definitely more than a pretty shell.

# 5

I don't know how I get through the next few hours, but I do know I'm thankful for that muffin. The energy that it takes to keep up with Mason as we work through the shots is something else. When the tight white t-shirt is tugged over his head, a whoosh of breath actually leaves my lips.

I was pretty certain that his body would be spectacular, but to actually see it in all its glory leaves me speechless. He seems to know how to work each important muscle – and there are plenty – to get the perfect form. I take shots from behind, with this head turned, admiring his broad shoulders and the perfect V of his back. He kicks his shoes off and reclines on the bed with his arms behind his head, and the sight of the muscles on the underside of his arms leading into his chest almost topple me. And his nipples. It wasn't an area I've thought about much on a man before, but everything about Mason is sexy. I'm pretty certain that I'd lick his armpit, that's how sexy he is.

I move in close, wanting to get some detailed shots before pulling back. "Can you open your belt and your jeans?" I ask as a rush of heat runs between my legs.

"Sure."

The clink of the buckle is music to my ears, and the sound of his zipper makes my heart skitter. He hooks a thumb into the waistband, pulling it down a little to reveal his tight black underwear, and I stumble over my own feet as I try to find a position to capture his perfection. I only have a few more shots of this, and then I'm going to need to move on to the ones without jeans.

"That's good," I say absentmindedly. Mason's eyes find mine through the camera, and it's a look that would sell a million books. A look that makes my upper lips prickle with sweat. Behind my camera, I still feel exposed.

He tugs his jeans down a little more, and I swear I see the bulge of his cock up high beneath the waistband of his tight shorts. Oh, my goodness. He's big all over.

"Good," I say again, my voice sounding breathy. His lips twitch with a smile, but he keeps his sultry expression in place. I snap away like a crazy person as Mason opens his jeans so wide, he might as well not be wearing any.

"Shall I take them off?" he asks.

"Sure."

That one word sounds half instruction, half pant, and I can't take my eyes off him as he eases those jeans over his muscular thighs until he's lying in just the underwear that leaves nothing to the imagination.

"Does that look good?" he asks, gazing down at himself. What kind of question is that? Of course it looks good. Does he not own a mirror? His eyes meet mine through the lens. "I mean, do you want me to move anything?"

"You could flex your right leg a little at the knee?"

"Okay. And my cock?"

My mouth makes a small shocked sound, and instinctively I lower the camera to look, even though it's a foolish and embarrassing thing to do. How can I tell a perfect stranger to adjust his junk? How could I watch him do that without my panties getting into an unacceptably messy state?

"It's errr…it's…" I blink slowly, trying to pull myself together. A strange part of me that I didn't know existed wants to tell him to hook a thumb in his waistband and pull so that I can see the thing that's teasing me behind too much thin fabric. It wants me to take his big cock into my palm and then into my mouth until my throat is gagging and my eyes are watering. My pussy feels hot and heavy between my legs and wet enough to slide down that cock with absolutely no problem.

Gone is the girl who felt like sex was just something to get through to keep a relationship going. Sex with Mason wouldn't be like that. It'd be as necessary as breathing, as vital as the blood pumping in my veins. I know this, and I don't even know his last name. I don't even know his favorite color or how his lips taste.

"It looks good," I splutter, and Mason makes a snorting noise as though I've amused him, but he doesn't want to make me feel bad by laughing out loud.

"I know it looks good," he says, "but is it in the right place?"

"Err…yeah. I guess."

"Well, you let me know if you want me to shift it…you know, to get the best angle."

Holy hell. I've never been with a man who had so much cock he could shift it for aesthetics, and to be honest, I can't believe that I'm actually having this conversation. All my idyllic days photographing the best of the world's sights are so far behind me. I suppose there are worse things to take pictures of, though.

I move a couple of steps back, inhale deeply and begin to take the shots. Mason moves fluidly, giving me plenty of variety, but the angle is wrong. At least, it's not the best that it can be.

There's a stepladder propped against the wall, and I lay my camera on the bed so I can get it set up. I need to be high to get some shots of Mason from above. I want him to look up at me with his sapphire eyes and those long lashes that cast the perfect kinds of shadows over his cheeks. I want to capture the undulations of his abdomen and the way his perfectly flat stomach dips in when he's horizontal, exaggerating the V of muscle leading down to his cock.

Climbing the steps, I feel shaky. My hands are slick with sweat against the hot body of my camera, and when I look through the viewfinder, I become even more of a hot mess. The angle I imagined is even better in reality, but it could be improved with just one little alteration.

I can't believe I'm actually going to say this, but I am. "Can you move your…your cock just slightly to the left."

Mason's hand slides over his stomach a little slower than necessary, and as he does exactly what I asked for as a thrill runs up the back of my neck and over my scalp. This moment will go down in my own personal history as the filthiest thing that has ever happened to me – watching his huge strong hand heft that long thick bar over at my order. Oof. I don't even know how to express how much it turns me on.

Who knew I had a bossy side? Who knew that I'd love it when a man acts on my instructions? Wow. This is a day of revelations, and not in the way I was expecting.

"Is that good?" he asks huskily. His eyes find mine through the camera, and it's as though he's licked a stripe between my legs. I actually jump.

"Yes. Perfect. Just like that," I reply through a throat tightened by lust.

I start to snap away, and Mason does his thing. All the while, I'm taking mental shots to keep me warm on the cold nights ahead. Seeing this man is a gift. More than a gift. It's like the images of Mason have wiped away some of the hurt I've been nursing.

Nate wasn't a fraction as impressive as this man. I need to realize that, although I'd built him into something huge in my life, he didn't deserve to inhabit that much space.

It takes the rest of the afternoon to get the shots that we need, and by then, I'm lightheaded from looking at Mason and from lack of food.

He ducks behind the screen to change back into his own clothes while I skip through the shots on my computer, and I'm so relieved to see that I've actually nailed it. I had so little confidence in myself, but with Mason's professionalism and my focus, this has actually been a great assignment.

I'm smiling when Mason appears, and his face breaks into a broad grin. "That's the happiest I've seen you all day," he says.

"The shots are awesome."

He slumps into the chair opposite me and puts his hands behind his head. "Of course they are. They're of me."

"Has anyone ever told you you're an arrogant ass?"

"Yep," he says without remorse. "But they've also said lots of good stuff too, so I tend to ignore the arrogant bit."

"Figures."

"So, dinner…" His eyes are full of challenge, and those dimples wink at me like the swinging chain of a hypnotist. How is it legal for a man to be so tempting? Mason needs a warning label.

"I don't think that's a good idea."

"That's because you're too hungry to make a sensible decision. I think I'm going to have to take over for your own good." He pulls his cellphone from his jacket pocket and starts dialing. "Yeah, can I get a table for two. Half an hour?"

"I…"

He puts his hand up to shush me. "Thanks. See you then."

I click through my shots, pretending to ignore him, pretending to be mad, but I'm not. That traitorous part of me is singing a happy song because for all Mason's arrogance, I get the feeling that he's actually a really good guy underneath.

I guess I'm about to find out.

# 6

I'm having dinner with Mason. Yes, it's against my better judgment, but as he fills my glass with more white wine, I find my judgment is the least of my concerns.

"So you've been traveling around a lot with your work," he says.

"Yeah. For twelve months. I only got back a couple of days ago."

"That must have been amazing. I've traveled, but it's mostly been assignments or short holidays. The assignments tend to involve seeing the insides of hotels and cabs, so nothing like the experiences you've had."

"I've been pretty lucky." As I say it, I see things through Mason's eyes rather than my own. I've been so sad about Nate and the regrets I have about how duped I've been that I've forgotten to appreciate the good.

"So, where's your favorite place?"

"It's so hard to choose. The world is so vast and all the countries in it so different. I don't think I could pick just one place."

"Tell me about some of the highlights."

"Well, I took shots at Abu Simbel in Egypt at sunrise. It's crazy just how big the temple is, and even crazier when you think they moved it to avoid the flooding caused by the Aswan dam. And Sukhothai in Thailand. The monumental Buddhas are breathtaking."

"Abu Simbel," Mason says. "I've never heard of it."

I reach to the floor to grab my purse and find my cellphone. I want to show him my favorite shot from that day. Maybe it'll inspire him to see it for himself. "Here, one minute." I fumble with my phone, swiping and swiping until I get to September. The shot I want practically jumps out of the phone. "Look…"

"Holy shit," he gasps, taking my phone and holding it close enough to study carefully. He uses his fingers to zoom in on the statues that flank the small doorway.

"It's the most amazing place. It was built so that two days a year, the sun rises in exactly the right place to illuminate all the statues at the back of the temple, all except the god of death who always remains in the dark."

"Seriously. It's so amazing that people back then were able to even think about that kind of thing, let alone build it."

I nod. "I thought exactly the same thing when I was there. Sometimes I wonder if we're really making progress as human beings. A lot of what was built in the past was way more beautiful than what is churned out today."

Mason hands me back my phone and takes a piece of bread from the basket on the table, tearing off a chunk. "It's money-driven now. Plus, there are a lot more safety regulations than there were back then. Thousands of men would have died laying the stones that built that temple."

"They still don't really know how they achieved it all. The stones weighed too much for men to lift, and they didn't have any power tools."

"It's a mystery." His eyes sparkle in the way that I've learned means he's going to say something cheeky. "I like mystery."

"What kind of mystery?"

"All mystery. Like, the way you dress. You cover everything you've got going on with so many loose layers of fabric. Unwrapping you would be like unwrapping a gift that had been packaged in an oversized box."

My cheeks heat at the thought of Mason peeling away my layers, and not just the clothes I choose to hide behind but the other complicated onion-layers that make me the person I am. Nate thought he knew me, but I never truly shared my hopes, fears, or dreams with him. He never asked, although he spoke plenty about his own.

I don't even know what it would feel like to be known like that. All the mystery stripped away. Anyway, it doesn't sound as though that's what Mason likes.

Men who like mystery get bored easily. Once they've seen everything that there is to see and know everything that there is to know, what else is there? Just the boredom that comes a year or so into a relationship.

"I think there's been enough unwrapping today."

"Can there ever be enough?" he laughs. "And anyway, I still have one layer left."

"And that layer shall forever remain a mystery."

The waiter chooses this exact moment to deliver a UFO-sized pizza to our table. I ordered a salad, which is placed in front of me. Although it looks perfectly appetizing, the smell of cheese and sausage wafts up my nose and sets off the saliva in my mouth. I'm like a dog at a barbecue.

Mason grabs a piece of pizza, folding the crust to give it some structure before he takes a big bite. I see the pleasure in his eyes. They practically cross with delight, and I look down at my salad, forking a piece of cucumber and popping it into my mouth. I don't even know why I ordered this. A habit I guess, born of Nate always "reminding" me that salad is healthy and dairy raises cholesterol. Plus, I knew he liked me super slim, so there was that too.

This isn't a habit I need to continue. As if Mason is reading my mind, he wipes his hands on his napkin and gestures to the pizza. "I order twice what I usually eat because it's so good, and I wanted you to share. Forget the salad. This restaurant is known for its pizzas, not it's lettuce, and you didn't eat any lunch. That bowl wouldn't satisfy a snail."

"It does smell good," I say, reaching tentatively to take a slice. The first bite is like slipping into cheese and tomato heaven. A moan rumbles in my throat, and my eyes roll. Seriously, this pizza is absolutely the best that I've ever eaten, and now I'm embarrassed. Why the hell didn't I just order this in the first place? I guess I've been adapting myself to fit in with Nate and what he wanted for such a long time that I didn't notice how much I lost of myself. How loud does a person have to be to silence another's internal voice?

Mason's so different. So encouraging of a way of being that is completely opposite to Nate's. Is that why I'm feeling drawn to him, despite my vow to steer clear of men for the foreseeable future? He's asked me so much about me, and I still know so little about him.

"So how long have you been modeling?"

"Five years," he says, shrugging. "It's not my passion, but it pays well, and it's easy work, as you saw today. I'm just using it as a means to an end, while I've got the body and the looks."

"I think you'll always have the body and the looks." I smile. "Before I came to the shoot, I did a ton of research on the romance book market. You know there's a whole genre of daddy romances with silver-fox covers. I can see you making a packet when you're in your forties and fifties."

"Well, that's a lot of years away. I'm hoping I might be living my dreams by then."

"What are your dreams?"

"I paint," he says simply. "I've always painted ever since I was a kid. I majored in fine art in college, but I haven't been able to make it pay. My dad...he thinks it's all a waste of time. He wants me to join his business, but I can't. I know myself well enough to be certain that I'd die cooped up in an office listening to people talk in boring clichés. I just can't find any enthusiasm for it, and he's disappointed."

"Well, I can understand him wanting to help you become successful, but it sounds as though he's going about it the wrong way."

Mason shrugs, tucking into his next pizza slice. "I don't share too much with him, so I can't place the blame solely at his feet. If he knew...if he saw what I was doing, then maybe he'd help."

"Maybe," I say. "My mom wasn't that keen on me traveling the world. She wanted me to set up a nice little studio and take shots of pregnant women and newborn babies and settle down. Sometimes it's hard for parents to accept that their kids aren't going to follow in their footsteps or live out the dreams they had for them. I guess until we're in their shoes, we won't know if we'll be any different."

Mason lowers his pizza and wipes his mouth with his napkin. His lips glisten with oil from the cheese, and when he licks them, the sight of his tongue sends a shiver through me. "You know what, Natalie... I'm pretty certain you're going to get it right. You're very emotionally intelligent."

I shake my head because he has no idea how foolish I've been. He has no idea how unobservant and trusting I've been when trust was the last thing Nate deserved. "I don't see what's in front of my face most of the time."

"And yet you put yourself in other's shoes so easily."

"Can you show me some of your art? I'd love to see it."

Mason reaches for his cellphone and starts to swipe through his images. I see his brows furrow as though he's not happy with what he's seeing, and I recognize the same self-criticism in Mason that I have myself. Look at today. I told Connie that I wasn't capable of making an excellent job of the shoot. She had more confidence in me than I had in myself.

Finally, he stops and passes me the phone, his hand hesitating over the pizza before I see his chest sink in resignation. He feels as though he's bearing his soul, and I guess he is in a way. When you are a creative, everything you produce contains a little piece of yourself. I'm not prepared for what is displayed on his screen.

It's spectacular. A giant abstract canvas in the kind of paint that creates texture. It's a naked woman lying with her back to the viewer, and everything about her is real and unreal all at the same time. "Wow," I say, shaking my head. "You are really talented."

“My bank account would tell you otherwise,” he chuckles wryly.

I wonder what part of Mason I'm looking at. There's something remote about the figure, something that speaks of pain and a lack of connection. Mason's point of view is outside that of the model.

“It's beautiful,” I say, meeting his eyes so he can see that I mean what I'm saying. “Hauntingly beautiful.”

“Thanks.” He reaches to take the phone, but I'm not happy with just seeing one image. I want more.

“Do you have any others on here? Can I see?”

He shrugs, and I can tell that there is nothing nonchalant about him giving me the freedom to roam his gallery this way, but I do it anyway.

“Wow.” It slips from my lips as I take in image after image of masterful, stunning paintings. Why he hasn't gotten an agent yet or had an exhibition somewhere high profile, I have no idea.

“You don't have to say that,” he says softly.

“I know I don't but...wow. You're going to be famous, Mason. Very, very famous. And it will have nothing to do with appearing on the front of millions of romance novels looking more well-endowed than any man has a right to. Just, wow.”

The snort that comes from Mason is one of pure shock and amusement. “Well, thank you. I think. For the lovely comments about my art and my...” He leans forward, looking from side to side to make sure he's not going to be overheard. “My cock. I wasn't sure you noticed. You did a good job of remaining professionally tight-lipped.”

“I think someone noticed in Alaska.”

He snorts again. “Now you're just flattering me.”

I shrug. "You obviously don't know how talented you are."

"Are we talking about painting now because I'm totally aware of how talented I am in other areas."

I shake my head, eyes flicking down to the pizza because I'm just not good at this kind of blatant flirting, although it would appear I feel somewhat comfortable branching into it with Mason. More comfortable than I've ever felt before.

"I'd love to see them in person," I say.

"Play your cards right, and you can see everything up close and personal."

I shake my head and roll my eyes. Now he's just getting cheesy. "Seriously. Maybe a morning sometime when you don't have a shoot."

"Fancy being a model for me? I'd happily immortalize you."

"Is that what they're calling it these days?"

Mason smiles broadly and leans back in his chair, those sparkling blue mischievous eyes sweeping over me approvingly. "You know what, Natalie? You are just a very interesting surprise, through and through."

"No one's ever called me a surprise before."

"That's because no one's ever taken the time to really see you, have they?"

Is it weird that Mason seems to know exactly what I've been thinking? He says I'm the one who puts herself in others' shoes, but he has a knack of reading me like an open book.

So much for closing myself off so nothing can hurt me again. I might as well be wearing clothes made of plastic wrap for all the concealing I'm doing.

"Some people never see what's right in front of them," I say.

"Can I take you somewhere when we've finished annihilating this pizza?"

I know saying yes is a mistake well before my mouth forms the word, but sometimes, even when we know we're on the path to ruination, we take a step forward regardless.

# 7

I don't know what I was expecting, but it wasn't this. Stuffed full of pizza, we stroll for a few blocks, making the easiest conversation I've ever had with a man. There's no posturing with Mason. No bravado. I don't get the feeling that I should be careful with what I say. I don't get the feeling that he needs constant flattery to keep him happy. The absence of all of these things is strange. Strange and tinglingly pleasant.

Eventually, Mason stops outside a small door and pulls a key from his pocket. For the first time, a rush of nervousness surges inside me. I don't really know this man. Not enough to be wandering around with him and entering strange buildings. He could be a Ted Bundy wannabe for all I know. Nobody knows where I am right now, or who I'm with, although Andre did see us leave together and the restaurant has a record of our booking. Am I a freak for thinking all this?

I'm worried until Mason smiles, and those dimples appear in full force. I'm an idiot for being swayed by such a little thing, but nothing about Mason has made me feel uncomfortable.

"I'll lead the way," he says, swinging the door wide open. "Just pull it closed behind you."

I do as he says and follow him up the stairs, watching his gorgeous ass moving from side to side. The stairs are steep and made of sharp concrete – not stairs that you would want to fall down – and they seem to go on forever. Where the hell is he taking me? All I know is that it's somewhere toward the top of this building.

At the top, there's another door that Mason unlocks. This time he holds onto the handle with some reluctance. He's brought me all this way, and now he doesn't want to let me in. What could he be so worried about?

"Just…I don't know why I brought you here but…"

"Do you want to go back?"

"No," Mason blurts. "It's just…" He eases open the door and flicks on the overhead lights.

It's his studio, and what a space it is. It must cost him a fortune, which must mean Mason comes from money. I'm pretty certain that he doesn't make that kind of money from modeling alone, and he's already indicated that he hasn't been successful at selling paintings.

Maybe I should be more reserved, seeing as we've only known each other since this morning, but my legs propel me into the middle of the cavernous room, and I pivot on my heel so I can take in each of the giant canvases. This is a treasure trove for an art lover, and I am one. Maybe all creatives are.

"This…you have to get these in front of the right people," I say. "Like this one…it's so…"

I don't actually have the words to describe the figure he's captured. The whole scene fills me with sadness that bubbles upward and constricts my throat. And isn't that how we know that art is great; when it elicits such an emotional reaction?

"You don't have to be so kind." Mason slides his hands into his pockets. "I know they're not gallery standard. Maybe they'd fit in some of the big offices in town, you know, to brighten the atrium."

"Don't even say that," I say. "These are not meant to be walked past by bored businessmen. They're meant to hang on the walls of those who truly appreciate them."

"Even my dad won't hang them in his house." I turn and find Mason's expression impassive. I know what he's said must hurt him greatly, but he won't show me that. Not yet. Maybe not ever.

"Well, your dad must be an idiot…and pardon the disrespect."

"He's a very clever man."

"Who is using his position to steer you away from your potential to do something that doesn't fit with his plan. Don't fall for that trick."

I keep walking, taking time to stand in front of each painting, and really soak it in. There are at least five that I'd love to own, not that I have a home to hang them in but whatever. Maybe I could buy them and put them into storage. I know they'll be worth a fortune in the future when someone with sense lays their eyes on them.

"Can I ask you something?" Mason's voice comes from close behind me, and I jump, not expecting him to be that near.

I turn, gazing up at him, the height difference between us feeling more marked in this position. "Sure."

"Can I draw you?"

Now it's my turn to lack confidence. The women in Mason's paintings are voluptuous, with long trailing hair and profiles that put mine to shame. The pixie haircut that I had on my travels to make self-care a little easier on the road suddenly makes me feel boyish rather than sophisticated. Anyway, Mason likes to draw nudes, and I'm not about to get naked in these harsh lights. He'd see every vein and scar, every imperfection.

"I don't think so."

"Please." He points to two chairs by the window. "You can sit there, just as you are. I just…there's something about you that I don't want to miss. A quality…" His eyes take on a dreamy glaze that mirrors the way I feel when I see true beauty worth capturing with my camera. Is that how he feels when he looks at me? Surely not.

"You must know plenty of women who'd look better in one of your paintings."

He shakes his head. "I just…please. It won't take long."

His please is what tips it. He's been so nice. I guess this is a good way of repaying kindness and pizza.

"Could I have a glass of water first?"

"Sure."

Mason disappears, and while he's gone, I pull out my cellphone and snap a few pictures of the paintings I love the best. I know just the person to send these to. Maybe I shouldn't interfere, but Mason seems to have had his confidence squashed, and I don't see him pushing himself forward in the way he should. Leaving these paintings to languish here would be a travesty.

When he returns, I sip the water and take a seat on the chair, and he slumps down too, grasping a piece of charcoal and a sketchbook. He rests it on his knee, and I'm reminded of the scene in the film Titanic, where Jack is getting ready to draw Rose. There's something so intimate about being studied so closely. Eyes become as tactile as fingers.

"Can you undo the top two buttons on your blouse? I want to see the column of your neck and your clavicle."

It's an innocent enough request, and although I like high-necked clothes, it's not because I'm scared of showing a little flesh. Unfastening the buttons brings up feelings of lost intimacy. When was the last time I undressed this way for a man? Have I ever? I can't recall.

I adjust the fabric so it falls to the sides, exposing the tan skin of my neck and chest. Mason bites his bottom lip in concentration, attacking the page in front of him with the charcoal in a way that appears almost violent. Surely he's not going to produce something lifelike working that fast. Maybe he's going for something really abstract. Maybe something surreal. I love Picasso and Dali. How awesome would it be to be immortalized into something so strange?

I watch him work, and every so often, his eyes meet mine. The connection is never accompanied by a smile, but there is a building level of electricity between us that feels dangerous. To be honest, any connection with a man would feel dangerous to me right now. I know it's not right to tar all men with the same brush, but I can't help feeling that I'm just not a good enough judge of character.

But maybe that's my problem. I've never just let my hair down and allowed myself to have fun without dragging my heart packed full of hopes into it. I've never sought pleasure for the sake of it. It has always been with the goal of a secure future in mind.

Well, I'm not ready to think about my future with someone else when I don't have anything in my diary past the weekend.

Mason pauses, then uses his finger to smudge the picture, his brow furrowed in concentration. If anything, it should be me capturing his beauty right now. I wish I had my camera in my hands, rather than where it's resting on the floor by the door.

When he finally stops, his eyes are as bright as the light refracted through a glass paperweight. "Perfect." He shakes his head. "I knew I had to draw you. I just…" He shakes his head again, standing with his pad and passing it to me. There's no embarrassment or reluctance to share what he's created, just pride and excitement, and I can see why.

He has captured me perfectly. More perfectly than I deserve. It's a smudgy and rough charcoal drawing, but the way he has the light reflecting off my cheekbones makes me appear almost ethereal. It's brilliant, and suddenly tears spring to my eyes. I blink and then gaze up at him, uncaring that he'll see the emotion radiating from me. Seconds thrill between us; moments where time slows and speeds in equal measure until I'm dizzy just from looking.

He takes my hand, his so warm and strong and mine so small. He leans down, bringing my hand to his lips. It's the most ridiculously romantic thing that anyone has ever done to me, so full of old-world chivalry that curtseying would seem the best response, except I'm still sitting down.

"Thank you," he says softly.

"What for?"

"Everything."

I want to tell him that it's me who should be grateful. He's been more than I could have hoped for; the antithesis of my previous relationship. He's opened my eyes to what is possible sometime in the future when I have my feet more firmly on the ground.

His lips are on mine before I can tell him any of that, though. His knee rests on my chair. His hands braced on the rounded arms as his mouth grazes mine so gently I feel it everywhere in the softest thrill of nerves. It's nothing like I expect and perfect all at the same time. No wet tongue stabbing blindly. It's like he's trying to discover me and waiting to know that I want to be discovered.

And I do. Oh, I do.

My heart skitters even though my mind is whispering to pull away. I should leave and return to the house I don't belong in. I should tell him that tonight was magical, but all good things have to come to an end, but my body doesn't agree. I want to find out things about Mason that would make me blush and things about myself too. Would it even be possible for me to take a man as big as Mason without wincing? Could I enjoy it? Would he make me feel different from Nate?

Sex is like dancing. Sometimes you work well with someone, as though your bodies know each other's language. At least, that's what I've heard. So far, my sex life has involved me speaking English and everyone else speaking Klingon. I have a feeling that Mason will dance with me like a professional. He'll lead, and I'll follow, and it'll be awesome.

I hope it'll be awesome.

He draws back, his eyes searching mine. "Was I wrong?" he whispers.

And just like that, I come to my senses. I can't do this crazy thing, no matter how much my body is crying out for it. I have to get out of here before I make a mistake I'm going to regret.

# 8

"We shouldn't," I say softly. Mason's eyes search my face, scanning for what he can decipher from my expression.

"Shouldn't?"

"I'm…it's not professional."

His mouth twitches. "I won't tell if you won't."

"That isn't really the point." He's still so close that I can smell the enticing fragrance of his cologne. So close that I could breathe in the scent of his skin if I just turned my head a little. My lips are still tingling from his kiss, my mind still spinning from his overwhelming closeness. I think he's going to try again. I think he'll be an ass and try to push past my pathetic-sounding excuse, but he doesn't. When he straightens up and lets out a deep exhale, the air around me seems to cool.

"I'm sorry," he says, sliding his hands into his pockets.

"It's okay," I say. "It was nice…"

"Nice?" Those full lips quirk again as though he's holding in a bubble of laughter at how prim I sound. No one wants to be described as nice. Nice isn't sexy. Nice isn't passionate. Nice is ordinary, and Mason certainly isn't that, but telling him how much I would love to have kissed him more wouldn't be the right thing to do. Mixed messages aren't fair, and I'm not a tease.

I shrug. "Sorry."

His head drops to the side as he regards me closely. "Why do you keep apologizing?"

That's a good question and not something I have ever really thought about. "What do you mean?"

"You don't need to apologize for saying what you want and don't want. That's your right as a human being. It's my duty to accept that is how you feel."

I feel my cheeks heating, and my eyes drop from his as his words settle inside me. When did I become the kind of woman who was always saying sorry? I guess I think that it's the right thing to do. It helps to make other people feel better, but the way that Mason has explained it shows how much I diminish my own worth.

My cheeks heat and I glance at the floor. "I think I should go."

"I'll come with you. Find you a cab."

It feels awkward, but it's a sensible idea at this time of night. I don't know this neighborhood well and have no idea about the kind of people or situations I could encounter out there. Plus, I have my camera equipment with me, which is my most expensive and treasured possession.

"Okay. Thanks."

He takes a step back so that I can stand. My knees feel weak from the kiss as I make my way to where I left my things. Mason holds out his hand for the camera bag, it's weight obvious from the way I'm standing. Such a gentleman.

It's awkward as we descend the stairs, and the unsettled feeling I have inside me seems to grow with every step. Outside, the night air is warmer than I'm expecting after the coolness of the loft space. Mason leads the way, and we pass stores and fast-food restaurants, as I follow him to a busier street where I have a chance of finding some transportation.

He tells me about the area, pointing out his favorite place to grab a beer and another where they serve great burgers. He smiles a lot, so different from how Nate would have reacted if I turned him down. There's no animosity or anger in Mason, no frustration or annoyance. He's done exactly what he said and accepted how I feel, and somehow that makes me want him more.

There's a freedom to being with Mason that I haven't encountered before, and as he shares more of what it's like to spend time in this neighborhood and paint, I find that I don't want to go home. All the worries I had about taking a frivolous step forward have disappeared, and all that's left is an overwhelming desire to make the most of this night with this man. I may never see him again, and I know that I'll regret getting in a taxi and driving away.

I turn my head, seeing how far we've now traveled from his loft, then on the corner, I spot a sign for a hotel.

There's no way that Mason is going to make another move on me, not after what I said. If I want this, I'm going to have to be the one to ask. It's not something I've ever done before, and I'm not that brave. My heart starts speeding as we get closer to the entrance. This is it. Walk past, and I'll miss the chance.

I can't do it. I don't have the courage that other women possess. Nate used to call me timid. It's such a pathetic word, and I don't want it to apply to me. I want to be the kind of woman who seizes the day, who makes the most of life's opportunities. I'm not going to fall in love with this man after one night of sex, but I will prove something to myself.

Something that needs proving.

"Mason." I stop, and so does he, turning to face me on the sidewalk. This is it. Can I do it? I gaze up at the illuminated sign. His gaze follows mine, flicking back with a quizzical expression.

"Are you okay?"

"Can we...can we go inside?" I cringe at the trepidation in my voice. So much for taking charge. I sound apologetic again. I'm seeking permission, and that's not how I want this to go. "I want to go inside...with you."

Mason's eyebrows practically hit his hairline. "You said that you didn't think it was a good idea for anything to happen between us. What's changed?"

"I...I..." I blink slowly like a rabbit in headlights. He's seriously asking me for an explanation? Of course he is.

"It's just that I want to make sure that this is what you want, not something you feel like you should do to please me."

"It's nothing to do with pleasing you," I blurt before realizing how terrible it sounds. A puff of amused air leaves Mason's nostrils. "I mean, it's what I want for me. If you want it for you, then..."

"I want it for me," he says softly. His hand reaches out to run his fingers over my hair. Time ticks as my heart pounds. He wants it, but we're still standing here. "Tell me again what you want."

My cheeks feel like they're on fire, and I'm dying a little more inside as every second passes. "I want you."

Mason's smile is as bright as the lights at the football stadium. His fingers find mine, lacing our hands together. "Come on then, Natalie. It's time for you to get what you want."

The rush of blood through my body is overwhelming. My mind can't really comprehend what is happening, and if it weren't for Mason we'd still be on the sidewalk. He talks to the receptionist, securing our room. When she hands him the key card and describes how to get there, I still don't take anything in. All I can think is that I'm doing this. I'm really doing this. It's really going to happen.

Then I remember that I'm wearing my plainest underwear and I haven't showered since this morning. Nate used to tell me to shower before bed if we were going to have sex, as though the scent of me wasn't appealing.

Mason gives my hand a squeeze as he leads me to the elevator. "Are you still with me?" he asks.

I nod, giving him a small nervous smile, my throat swallowing involuntarily with nerves.

As the doors close, he moves closer, brushing his thumb over my bottom lip, his eyes darkening. "This is going to be…phenomenal," he says.

Phenomenal. That's not a word that anyone has ever used about me in any context.

The elevator pings, and the doors grind their way open. Mason glances from left to right before leading me in the direction of room 77. Double the luck. As the latch clicks open, my heart skitters, and when the door closes behind us, I feel almost faint.

Mason puts my camera bag on the desk and pulls his phone, keys, and wallet from his pockets, laying everything neatly. I stand holding my purse in front of me like a shield, but Mason gently takes it from me, resting it next to his things. I don't know what to do with myself, especially when Mason looks at the bed.

"It looks comfortable."

"It does."

"We're going to play a game," he says, a smile playing across his lips and those dimples flashing for just a second.

"What game?" I hope he's not into anything kinky because I'll be out of this room in a flash.

"It's called 'Natalie's in charge.'"

"What?"

He cocks his head to the side. "You're going to tell me what you want, and I'm going to give it to you."

My heart sinks. This is not what I imagined being with Mason would be like. He's big and strong with lots of confidence in his body. I had visions of him picking me up and fucking me against the wall, of flipping me over and grabbing my hair. I wanted the full-on alpha dominant thing, but now he wants me to be boss. I'm not boss material.

"I…why?"

"Because I think you need to get better at asking for what you want."

"Isn't that what I just did downstairs?"

He smiles and puts his hand on my arm. "And how difficult did you find it?"

"Almost impossible." I shake my head, not believing I can really do what he's suggesting. I don't use dirty words. I don't know how to be a woman who asks a man to please her. My standard approach in bed is to follow the lead and hope that the man I'm with knows what he's doing. If they don't, I've never been okay with giving directions.

"What do you want me to do?" His hand lifts my chin so that I'm looking him dead in the eye. Everything else slips away until all there is is me and him and the blood rushing in my ears.

"Kiss me," I whisper.

When he does it is just as it was at his studio, soft, teasing, and mesmerizing. I'm lost in the movement of his lips against mine, the slide of his tongue, the feeling of his hand moving down my back until it rests at my waist. Oh God, I've never been kissed like this. It's as though he's feeling me out, learning what I like, pushing forward and pulling back until I'm leaning into him, needing more.

Heat rushes between my legs, my pussy becoming, a heavy and aching thing that wants Mason more than it's ever wanted anyone before.

"What else?" he whispers.

I cringe, the next step seeming harder to ask for than a simple kiss, but I want more, and if I'm going to get it, I'm going to have to be brave. "Take this off," I say, tugging at the hem of his tee.

He tugs it over his head in that way you see on sexy cologne adverts, with just one hand grabbing at the back of the neck, and I almost pass out. It's stupid because I've spent a lot of today photographing the perfect body that's revealed in that one movement, but it doesn't make viewing Mason in all his glory any easier. Damn. He is finer than fine. He tosses the shirt onto a chair and hooks one thumb into the waistband of his jeans. My fingers itch for my camera. This would make for a perfect shot with just a little mood lighting, but Mason isn't here to pose. He's waiting for instruction.

"And the rest." It slips out, and my hand clamps over my mouth as though it did something bad, but Mason just looks pleased. I didn't see him undress this way today. That show mostly took place behind a screen. I get the treat now, though. Shoes and socks first, then he unbuckles his belt, pops the buttons on his jeans, and pushes them down until they're a puddle on the floor, and I'm left with just Mason in form-fitting underwear that leaves nothing to the imagination.

His hand goes to his cock, squeezing gently once, as though he needs just a little relief. "These too?"

All I can manage is a nod, and when he pushes them down over his muscular thighs, and I see his cock for the first time, an audible gasp leaves my lips.

Mason is BIG. Really BIG. So big that I can't take my eyes off it.

I stare and stare, feeling hotter and hotter until Mason clears his throat, and I'm jolted from my daze.

"Do you like looking at it?" His question isn't voiced in a sexy way. He really wants to know.

"Yes. It's…" I don't have the words for the impact it's making on me, the way it's making me feel. There's something primal that I would never have guessed was lying dormant inside me – a need to be claimed by a man who can really make me feel it.

Mason wraps his hand around his cock and strokes up and down, and the sight hits me between the legs. Watching him…it's so unbelievably intimate, but just as I'm really starting to enjoy it, he stops.

"What next, Natalie?"

His eyes challenge me, pushing, prodding, making me step outside my comfort zone into a new way of being – an assertive way of being.

"Sit on the chair," I say. "And carry on doing what you were doing."

"You want to watch me?" When I nod, Mason's smile is intrigued. I wonder what he thought this would be like. Did he expect this or something different? I guess the not knowing is part of the appeal, but I don't think this is about him at all. This is all about me.

As Mason sits on the bedroom chair in the corner, I perch on the bed. He licks his palm in a slow swipe that I feel over my clit, then uses the slickness of his saliva to lubricate his pulls. His hand is big, but it doesn't obscure his cock. I moisten my lips, eyes focused as his hand rotates slightly on each downward pass, the wide, rounded head of his cock coming into view like the best kind of tease.

How would it feel for that thing to push inside me? Would it hurt? Would it stretch me? Would I still feel the intrusion the next day?

I glance up at Mason's face, and even in the low light of the room cast from the bathroom, I can see his cheeks are flushed. He's really aroused now, but I don't want him to come, as sexy as that would be. I swallow as an image rushes through my mind of his head thrown back in ecstasy, and his hand covered with cum. Not yet. I want that all for myself.

My blouse is still unbuttoned at the top, so it doesn't take long for me to unfasten it fully. My bra is plain cream satin, but Mason doesn't seem to mind. He rests his hands on his thighs and watches me slide the fabric over my arms and then stand so I can push my cotton pants to the floor.

My face feels hotter than it's ever been, but it's not because of Mason. I actually feel more comfortable standing half-naked in front of him than I ever did with Nate. There's no judgment with Mason. He is what he is and I am what I am. The heat comes from taking a step closer to where this is leading and knowing what I want to ask him for next. Can I do it? I don't know.

"I'm going to go to the bathroom to freshen up," I say. I have to do that before I ask. It's what's expected.

"No," Mason says, and it's firm enough that I stop in my tracks.

"What?"

"You don't need to freshen up," he says. "Just tell me what you want next." He moistens his lips like he's hoping I'm going to ask for something involving his mouth. It's what I want, but can I ask?

I step closer to him, trying to remember the last time I had an orgasm and finding that I can't. I'd pushed all expectations of that aside for a long time, but I don't want to do that with Mason. I want to believe that he'll understand my body enough to make me come. Hooking my thumbs at the sides of my panties, I start to push them down, but his hands gently pull mine away, and he takes over. It's so much sexier for him to undress me, and he takes his sweet time. He kisses my stomach, and I gasp as my panties slide over my ass, and I'm revealed to him. His hands stroke up the back of my thighs, stopping at my ass and squeezing gently. He kisses along my stomach, and I feel him inhaling against my skin as though he's searching for my scent. Is that why he didn't want me to wash? Does he find it a turn-on?

"Tell me what you want," he murmurs into the soft hair at the apex of my thighs. He's so close to my pussy that it would take nothing for him to lick me there, but I have to ask first. His game isn't going to end until I've asked for it all, but this is harder than everything that has come before.

"Make me come," I whisper.

"How?" he kisses my stomach again, teasing me to the point that my knees weaken. I don't know how much longer I'm going to be able to stand like this. "With your mouth."

As though he read my mind, he suddenly stands, scooping me up around the ass and carrying me to the bed. He kneels on the mattress, lowering me carefully, his hands pushing my knees wide, his crystal blue eyes on my pussy. His chest rises and falls, hands sliding up the inside of my thighs, thumbs gently parting me before he lowers his face. Oh God, the heat of his tongue is too much, the roughness over my already swollen clit making me jump. I drop my arm over my eyes because seeing him devouring me is too much, and he does. He eats me out like I'm the most delicious dessert, flicking at my clit until I'm trembling, licking hungry stripes, teasing at my entrance. Mason is a man who loves pussy. There's no trepidation in his approach, no hint of being grossed out or only doing it because it's expected. And he knows what he's doing because I'm so wet I can feel it trickling between the cheeks of my ass and so close that I'm twitching. "Fuck," I gasp, "Don't stop." But I didn't need to say it because there is no stopping Mason. He's a man on a mission, and that mission is me.

"Oh…oh…." I dig my fingers into the comforter, trying to find purchase as he lifts one of my legs higher and slides a thick finger just inside me, pushing upward against my G-spot. Just like that I'm coming and coming and coming, bright lights flashing before my eyes. I put my hand on the top of his head, holding him still because there is no way I can take any more. No way in hell.

But of course, there's so much more to come, if I just have the courage to ask.

# 9

How long should it take for a person to come down from an orgasm? I think I'm taking too long. Mason's been hard for ages. He teased himself to the point of shaking and licked me until the top of my head almost blew off. He must be about to die of frustration, but when I open my eyes and gaze down at him, he looks really pleased.

"There you are," he says. "I thought maybe I broke something."

I shake my head, swallowing against the lump that's formed in my throat because he couldn't be more wrong. If anything, he's put a little piece of me back together. I blink, not wanting tears to glaze my eyes. I touch his face, the scruff of his beard bristly against my palm. Mason closes his eyes like a cat who wants to purr, and there's no urgency in his actions. No pressure to move on to his release like I've experienced in the past.

"I've wanted to do that all day," he murmurs as he turns into my palm and presses a kiss into the center. I make a snorting noise. "You don't believe me?"

"I haven't exactly been dressed to attract the opposite sex."

"And that's what made me wonder what it'd be like to unwrap what's underneath all that hippie chic. You were wound up so tight…so professional, I just wanted to see you let go."

"Now, you've seen it."

"Yes, I have, and I want to see it again."

He raises up on his arms, looming over me, the weight of his cock on my stomach, making me look down. It's like a baton or a baseball bat, imposing in length and girth. The cock of a man with an immense physical presence. The cock of a man waiting for my instruction.

"I'm on the pill," I say. "But I think we need to be careful."

"I was tested after my last relationship. I haven't been with anyone since," Mason says. Do I believe him? I do, actually. Everything about how he's treated me today tells me that he's a man of his word.

"Okay," I say.

"Okay, what?" He dips down to kiss the corner of my mouth, and I can taste the smile on his lips.

"Okay, you'd better get on with it then," I say.

The chuckle that rumbles from the man on top of me is deep and loud. He nuzzles my neck, his laughter tickling the sensitive skin below my ear. "Yes, ma'am."

He doesn't need to take hold of his cock to get it in the right position. He simply cants his hips until it's pressing against my slippery entrance and pushes forward, his eyes never leaving mine.

"Ready?"

I want to say no. How could anyone be ready for what Mason's got going on? It's daunting and intriguing in equal measure. Just the blunt head feels too much for me, forget the rest of it.

I nod once, bracing myself as Mason's pretty eyes watch me. "It'll be okay," he says. "I'll go slow."

Slow. I don't know if that will be any better. Maybe he just needs to shove it in so I can get past the nervous anticipation that has my clit starting to throb again. Oh. My. Goodness. I pant as he rests the weight of his pelvis a little lower, and starts to push inside me. At first, it feels like nothing is working. I'm wet as a river, but it's so big. Then I feel the stretch as my pussy starts to accept him, and what a stretch it is.

I've heard other women talk about men with big dicks but never understood the appeal. It's just for porn stars, and most of them aren't that attractive. Men want to see little women fucked by men who are hung like horses, and the women don't really seem to be enjoying themselves. Everything is fake, the cries of pleasure staged and unbelievable.

But now I get it. As Mason pulls back a little and pushes forward again, I totally get it. My eyes roll as he flicks my bra open with one motion and palms my breast. I totally get it as he sucks hungrily on my nipple, moving ever deeper as my whole body feels like it's spreading wide to accommodate him. Is it strange that I feel that no one else will ever possess my body this way? No other man is going to have what it takes. A shiver rushes across my skin because it feels too good, and that's amazing and terrifying in equal measure.

This is just a one-night thing. I'm pretty certain that's what Mason wants, and it's what I went into this thinking I wanted. But now, the thought that this might be the only time I ever feel this way fills me with panic. How do you go back to eating crackers when you've had the most delicious steak? How do I go back to eating salad after pizza? Reluctantly, that's how, with longing for days that have past and will never be relived.

But I need to live it first. I need to be present at this moment with this amazing man who has forced me to see myself in new ways; lit up by an invisible force in his drawing, and capable of asking for things that would never have left my lips before tonight. Isn't that what we all long to find? The person who helps us to live a better life as the best version of ourselves that we can be?

I grasp his shoulder, letting out my breath slowly as he fills me so completely that I don't feel like I can move. His lips find mine, teasing with soft kisses so that I relax enough to take even more. He's so deep that I feel an ache, but then he withdraws just a little, and it's pure pleasure.

Running my fingers down his back, I can feel his muscles shift as he grinds into me. My palms seek out the roundness of his ass, gripping hard and forcing him closer. He fucks me harder, the pressure perfect against my clit and deeper inside me too.

I've never come from penetrative sex, so the building of an orgasm feels totally unreal. It's a different feeling, being filled so completely combined with the escalating pleasure. His teeth nip at my nipple, and I cry out, moving my hips, so he's exactly where I need him to be, and that's all it takes.

I cry out, and it's the first time I've heard myself make that noise. I thought it was just a thing that people faked to make their partner feel good, not something that wells up from deep inside a person so fast that it just can't be held inside anymore. I feel Mason swell inside me, the very idea that could be possible blowing my mind.

"Fuck," he mutters, his hand going beneath my leg and pushing my knee upward, moving even deeper. I gasp, an ache spreading through me as I feel him let go.

The moment is overwhelming; witnessing a strong man made so weak by my body. He buries his face in my neck, his breath gusting hot against my skin, and I stare at the ceiling, warmth spilling through me. So this is what it's supposed to be like. The overwhelming feeling of mutual release is everything that I've been missing.

But it's not only that.

Mason handed me control. He made me ask for what I wanted, and it's that that has me reeling. It feels amazing to have been so brave. It feels amazing to have been given exactly what I requested. The sex was perfect. Absolutely perfect.

Mason pushes up on one arm, using his other hand to stroke my hair back from my forehead. His mouth forms a lazy smile, his eyes still dazed from his orgasm.

"Well, that was a great surprise. I was not expecting you to change your mind."

"I wasn't expecting it either," I say. "I don't do this."

"You don't have to explain yourself. I don't need you to tell me why. I'm just happy you did."

He leans in to kiss my lips, and it feels more intimate than it should, and I don't know how but somehow Mason gets hard again, and rather than me getting up to leave and going back to the beach house, I stay, and find that he shows me even more of what I've been missing.

Of course, I have to ask for everything that he gives me, and I get it all. Sex up against the wall, from behind while he grips my hair in his fist, and when he's done ruining me for any man in my future, Mason falls asleep, and so do I.

Well, it was inevitable, wasn't it?

# 10

I know that he's gone as soon as I wake. The room has a stillness about it that it could never have with Mason in it. My eyes are bleary as I scan the room, finding my clothes have been placed neatly over the back of the chair, and my purse and camera bag are arranged on the desk.

The only sign that Mason was ever here is a dip in the pillow next to me and a sticky sore feeling between my legs. Oh, and an ache in my heart that was there because of Nate but is now less about him and more about the fact that I won't get to kiss Mason good morning or hear his deep laugh again.

Shit.

I touch my lips, the feeling of his kiss still fresh enough in my memory to send a shiver up the back of my neck. I lift the covers and gaze at my body, which withstood so much pleasure last night that I'm in awe. Still the same small breasts and protruding hip bones, except this morning my nipples are tipped with rose pink caused by Mason's mouth and teeth, and my clit is still swollen. I press my hand between my legs, remembering the first lick of his tongue there. Lower, my entrance is still wet from his cum. It's not something that I've ever really liked before, but today I love it so much I run my fingers through it and bring them to my lips. I smell him, the masculine scent of his claiming. I don't want to shower straight away. I want to keep him with me for the rest of the day. I wriggle from beneath the covers, and pad across the soft carpet to search out my phone. The light of the screen hurts my eyes, and the number of missed calls on the home screen is staggering.

Shit again!

I forgot that Mom would be expecting me home. I'm not used to having to answer to her and forgot to let her know I was staying out. She must be going out of her mind imagining me in a ditch or something.

I dial her number, feeling the familiar panic of having to deal with her overly emotional responses to everything. "Natalie. Thank goodness. Where are you?"

The guilt feels as thick as tar inside me because she sounds close to tears, and I haven't been fair at all. "I'm sorry, Mom. I stayed out with a friend, and time got away from me. I should have called."

"You should have," she says. "I was really worried. And you're late for brunch."

"Brunch?" I look at the time on the screen and find that it's 11 am. How the hell did I sleep in this late? It's pitch black in the room, and I'm still jetlagged, so I guess that it explains it.

"Where are you? I'll send Daryl to collect you."

"Okay. Can you send me his cell and I'll send him my location? That'll be the easiest thing."

Mom sighs as though I'm being difficult. She's never been great with technology, so she probably imagines what I'm asking her to do is very complicated.

"We'll wait for you. Brunch will have to become lunch."

"You don't have to Mom. Honestly. You and Conrad eat. I can grab something here."

"We have guests, honey. We'll see you soon."

She hangs up the phone without elaboration, and I stare at the screen, waiting for the number. When I've arranged my ride, I look around the room, hoping to find a little note from Mason with his number, but there's nothing. For all his sensitivity toward me, he was fast to leave this all behind. So fast, I feel the burn of his rushed departure.

I promised myself I would take last night for what it was – two people coming together for a night of spectacular passion – but it's harder than I told myself it would be. Running my fingers through my hair, I sigh. Mason will always be a tantalizing memory of something perfectly right but totally enigmatic.

In the bathroom, I splash my face with water and run my wet hands through my bed-hair. My green eyes look ridiculously bright in the LED light shining from above the mirror, and my cheeks have a pretty flush to them. It just shows what good sex can do to a person. I glance at the luxurious shower and consider the guests who are joining us for lunch. I decide to just run a washcloth over my top half but leave Mason right where he is between my legs. It'll be my delicious secret to keep for just a little longer.

I dress quickly, feeling strangely uncomfortable in my own clothes. As I glance at myself in the mirror, I feel too shrouded by the volume of loose fabric. Maybe I need to update my wardrobe now that I'm not on the road in Asia anymore.

My camera equipment is heavy on my shoulder as I descend in the elevator. Heavier, when I remember the shots I have of Mason that I will need to review and edit before sending them to the publishing house. Not only am I carrying the memory of him on my body and in my mind but also the images of him that set me on fire. Looking through them is going to be sweet torture.

Gregory is waiting for me on the corner, and I jump in, eager to pull out my camera and gaze at Mason again. The first image to appear is the last I took, and it's the most erotic. His eyes are fixed on the camera as though he is looking right into my soul. That body that wrecked me so perfectly is positioned for maximum impact, and the cock that I can still feel inside me is dormant but still unbelievable.

Wow.

I stifle a giggle that bubbles up inside me. If Connie knew what I did with this Adonis of a man, she'd have kittens. She'd be getting me to say a million thank yous to her for putting me forward for the job. She'd be asking for absolutely every filthy detail, and I'd be tempted to share because I've never before had sex I've been able to rave about.

As we pull into the driveway, there are three cars I don't recognize. Gregory opens my door and retrieves my bag from the trunk. I make my way to the front door, feeling a little like a teenager doing the walk of shame.

I'm just about to ring the doorbell when the front door opens, and instead of Mom waiting to chastise me, it's Mason standing in the doorway with a very shocked look on his face.

# 11

"Natalie. What are you doing here?"

"This is where I live," I say. "What are you doing here?"

"You live here?" Mason's face is the picture of surprise, as I suppose is mine. When a man climbs out of your bed after sex and leaves without saying goodbye, you're certainly not supposed to be faced with the indignity of bumping into him in your own home.

"Ah…there she is." My mom's voice echoes in the vast hallway, and then she appears behind Mason. "Natalie. Come in quickly and put your things in your room. The food has been waiting long enough."

"Natalie…" I see the moment that Mason registers that the Natalie whose pussy he was licking a few hours ago, is the same Natalie who is Sandra's daughter.

But who is Mason?

"And you've met Mason. That's good."

I hold out my hand and look Mason in the eye. "Nice to meet you, Mason." My brain searches for his surname, which was on the job details for the photoshoot. Mason Hopegood. Maybe he's the son of a friend of the family.

Mason shakes my hand, his own feeling hot and a little sweaty.

"You just have Max and Miller to meet now."

Max and Miller?

"Max and Miller Banbury. My brothers," Mason says, and my stomach almost drops to the floor. I knew Conrad had three sons, but I wouldn't have been able to recall their names from a conversation over a year ago. And Mason must go by a "stage name" in his work life.

My cheeks flame as Mason squeezes my hand in his. It's patently obvious that neither of us knew, and both of us are ridiculously uncomfortable.

I slept with my stepbrother last night.

My stepbrother.

Isn't that illegal? It certainly feels like it should be.

Awkward doesn't even come close to describing the awful creeping feeling of shame that prickles the hairs on my arms. This man has tasted me intimately. He's seen all of my most private places. He knows how I sound when I come. He slept by my side and left me without a second glance.

I have his cum in my pussy FFS. My resistance to showering this morning suddenly feels like a terrible idea.

And now I have to eat brunch/lunch with him as though none of that happened. I don't know if I can do it.

"You're Mason Banbury?" Mason nods, his jaw ticking with what looks like annoyance, and I know I have to get away from him as quickly as I can.

I brush past him, smiling with as much fakeness as I can muster, so Mom doesn't wonder what all the weirdness is about. "I'll be down in a minute."

I jog up the stairs, not looking back, and hurry down the corridor to my room. When I've closed the door behind me, I rest against it, swallowing down all the strange feelings I have rushing around inside me.

Mason is Conrad's son.

I laugh manically because this is like the worst thing that could have happened. It's going to be the one-night-stand that never goes away. Every time I see him, I'm going to remember. Every time he sees me, he's going to be pissed. It's so obvious that he's angry that I'm here. He wanted just to leave me behind and never look back, and that makes me sad. All the good feelings I had about him are tainted. That one flicker of his jaw painted over a whole night of gloriousness with a thick black brush of regret.

I didn't want what happened between us to be about regret. I have enough of that haunting me with Nate still in the back of my mind. This was supposed to make me feel better – the awakening of a powerful, more assertive version of myself.

There's no time to shower, but I wish I could. It would definitely make me feel better to wash Mason away.

I rest my bags on the bed and glance in the mirror. Rather than glowing, my face looks sweaty, and my eyes are circled by dark rings. I reach for my make-up and do what I can to make myself more presentable. Then I find a floaty summer dress in my closet. The white embroidered fabric sets off my tan skin and makes my hair look a softer shade of summer-highlighted blonde. It's nice enough, but not too much. I don't want Mason to think that I'm dressing up for him, although I am a little. Of course I am. I want him to look at me and think about what he's missing by being a douchebag who didn't leave me his number and is now related to me.

My stomach rolls; part hunger and part sick at the thought.

What do I call him? My brother. That feels seriously wrong.

I know Mom must be almost apoplectic by now, so I dash down the stairs, running my hands through my hair to give it some tousled charm. At the bottom of the stairs is a man who looks so much like Mason I almost stop in my tracks. It's not him because this man has tattoos all over his arms. His blue eyes meet mine, and I see the surprise there. I must look like a crazy nymph appearing in billowing white fabric with bare feet.

"Hey," I say. "I'm Natalie. We're late for lunch."

"Yeah," he says, his voice the same as Mason's too. "I'm Max. We'd better get a move on."

I follow Max through the house to the large wooden-decked area that overlooks the sea. Mom is there with Conrad, Mason, and the other Banbury brother, who would be impossible to tell from Mason if I didn't already know what he was wearing. My God…identical triplets. I don't think I even knew that was a thing. As the man I'm assuming to be Miller's eyes meet mine, I'm pretty certain that Mason has told him about last night. There's a filthy gleam in his baby-blues that makes me want to punch him in the face, and I glance at Mason, finding him looking down at the napkin that rests formally on his plate.

A light summer breeze drifts across the deck, ruffling my hair and distracting me for a moment. My eyes drift to the view and I'm completely mesmerized at the beauty of it. The deck is surrounded by a modern glass balustrade, which allows an uninterrupted vista of the golden sand and turquoise water. The waves lapping at the coast are calling my name – any frustration at being in this strange house that isn't my home drifts away. I may not be here for long, but I'm going to make the most of it, for sure. If I can get past this awkwardness, that is.

"Natalie, come and sit beside me," Mom says, waving at the chair. Conrad is at the head of the table. I'll be sitting directly opposite Mason, which isn't ideal, but at lunch for six, I was never going to be far from him. Max takes the seat at the opposite end to his dad, and a moment of strange silence hangs over us.

"It's so nice to finally have you all together," Conrad says, raising a glass of what looks like champagne. Of course, it would be champagne. "Natalie is finally back from her travels, and my sons are all in one place for a change."

"It's marvelous," my mom says, raising her glass. I glance in front of me and find that mine is filled too. Are we making a toast?

"To family," Conrad says, prompting a strangulated sound from Mason. His eyes meet mine, and they look pained.

"To family," Miller says with another wide-eyed smile.

"To family," Max says. Maybe he doesn't know our secret because he just sounds a little bemused. It is a strange toast because family is one thing that we aren't. This is just too strange.

Food is brought to the table by a man dressed in smart attire. It's like being in a luxury hotel, not a home. At least, not a home I'm used to.

Mason, Max, and Miller grew up with this.

That makes me feel strange. Before I knew who Mason was, I just assumed he was like me. An average boy from an average family, but the Banburys are anything but ordinary. They're wealthy and privileged. They will have had a completely different upbringing. No wonder Mason has a loft space like a well-known artist. His dad must be paying.

The starter is smoked salmon and avocado with a delicious lemony dressing. Conrad is loud and appreciative, complimenting the chef and my mom for putting together a great menu. Things have changed a lot for her. Now all she has to do is organize what other people are doing in the household – no more rustling up mac and cheese for Sandra Banbury.

"So, Natalie, you must tell my boys what you've been up to. Natalie is a photographer."

"Really," Max says. "What do you photograph?"

I avoid looking at Mason because I know I'll blush. "I've been focusing on travel photography for the last year."

"Really? Where?"

"I've been all over. South America, Africa, and South East Asia."

Max nods, taking a sip of his champagne. "And where was your favorite?"

"I don't think I could pick just one place. The world is so interesting. There is beauty everywhere."

"I've always wanted to go to Egypt," he says.

"He always loved watching documentaries," Conrad adds.

"And our tutor was a professor of ancient history."

"Your tutor?"

Max smiles. "We were homeschooled for quite a lot of our childhood."

"Well, I could pay for the best, and there were three of them at the same age."

"Wow. That must have been different."

I find myself searching out Mason then. He's looking directly at me, but as soon as my eyes meet his, he looks down at his food again.

"It wasn't great," Miller says. "Professor Walters was a crusty old man. He used to bore us to tears."

"Don't say that," Conrad says. "He was a great man."

"Was," Miller says. "Exactly. He was so old he's already dead."

"I think what Miller is trying to say is that having an ancient man as your only teacher and your two brothers as your only classmates isn't the education he would choose now," Mason says.

"Well, children don't get to choose and look at you. You've all graduated. You're all educated men, although you might not always look that way."

Conrad looks directly at Max's tattoos, giving a distinct impression that he doesn't approve.

"Natalie had the normal high school and college experience," Mom says. "I always had to work."

"You've raised an amazing woman," Conrad says, laying his hand on Mom's arm.

I know he's trying to be kind to his wife, but I'm still flattered.

"So, just travel photography?" Miller asks.

"Natalie had a shoot just yesterday, didn't you darling?"

"Yes." Why the hell is Mom getting involved and making this difficult.

"Ah…what did you shoot yesterday?"

"It was a shoot for a book cover."

"Really. Horror? Thriller?" Miller is trying to stifle a smile but failing. He's enjoying every minute of the cringe-fest he's creating.

"Romance," I say, putting a big bite of food into my mouth. Hopefully, he'll get the hint that I don't want to talk anymore.

"Really. That sounds like fun. Was it a couple?"

I chew, my building annoyance channeling into my grip on the cutlery.

Maybe Max can sense something's going on because he asks his dad something about the stock market, and Conrad begins a long explanation of market movements, and Miller has to give up his attempts to expose Mason and me. My appetite has disappeared, though.

I gulp champagne to wash down the fish and dab at my mouth, feeling sweat prickling under my arms. Miller could tell his dad what Mason and I did. He could cause so many problems. Maybe it would spoil things between Mom and Conrad. Maybe Conrad wouldn't want me to stay here anymore.

I don't take in much of what's going on around me after that. The waiter clears the plates and brings out the main course of grilled squid and steamed vegetables. I usually love squid, but today it feels like rubber in my mouth. Even the dessert of berry pavlova doesn't appeal.

I've messed up badly. Again. No decisions I ever make where men are concerned are good decisions.

After lunch, I make my excuses and find my way down to the beach to clear my head. The sand is soft between my toes and I hitch my dress into one hand and hold my sandals in the other so that I can paddle in the shallows. It reminds me of my time on so many other beautiful beaches around the world. All of those memories are now bittersweet.

I haven't made it far before I hear my name being called. When I turn, I see Mason jogging down the beach behind me. My feet propel me forward but slowly. I'm still angry and disappointed at his behavior but also intrigued at why he's come to find me. Maybe I'll get my opportunity to voice my feelings, and that will make me feel better. Bottled up emotions are the hardest to deal with.

"What is it, Mason?" I say coldly as he catches up to me.

"I'm…I'm sorry for the way Miller was behaving."

"Miller?" I shake my head. "Miller is a grown man who'll need to apologize for himself. As should you."

Mason reaches out to catch my elbow. "Why do I need to apologize?"

"Because you left this morning without saying goodbye."

"I had to get here for brunch," Mason says. "And you were sleeping so heavily. I tried to wake you, but…" He shrugs and I feel my face scrunching with disbelief. Is he really telling me that I was impossible to wake?

"But what?"

"I thought maybe you were pretending to be asleep so you didn't have to go through the awkwardness of the morning after."

I blink slowly, my eyebrows raising because either Mason is a master twister of reality or he just admitted to thinking I wouldn't be interested in anything other than a one-night stand with him. Is he serious? Has he not seen himself? If he really thought that, maybe he's not as confident in himself as I thought. He certainly lacks self-belief about his artistic abilities, and I can see why Conrad might not have been the most encouraging father.

"You were disappointed when I wasn't there?"

I shrug as though none of this means anything to me, but just by making an issue about this, I've shown that I'm bothered. "It was what it was. And that's the end of it, even if our parents weren't married."

"What's that got to do with it?"

I can't believe Mason's flippancy. Does he not get how weird this whole situation now is? "You're my stepbrother," I say.

"Yeah…this is a strange development."

"I don't think that strange covers it. Awkward might be better."

"What's so awkward? So we had sex. We're grown. We're free to make our own decisions. And it seemed like a pretty great decision for me."

He looks at me pertinently, as though he's asking me if I regret what we did. "It was amazing," I say.

"Amazing enough to do it again?"

I drop my skirt and push my windswept hair from my face. "I don't think your dad and my mom would think that was a good idea."

"Well, I wasn't planning on inviting them to watch."

"Very funny." I look back at the beach house, our shared family home. Sex shouldn't fit there, and I'm not ready for anything more than what I asked for last night.

"I like you," Mason says. "And I think you like me?"

Now there's a question that I'm pretty sure he's using to back me into a corner, but I'm not going to fall into that trap. "I just broke up with someone. It's not the right time, and don't think that this is the right place."

Mason puts his hand on my arm. "I'm sorry," he says. "Break-ups are hard, and I get why you think that all this makes things complicated. But you're running before walking. This doesn't have to be anything more than what you want it to be…what you need. And no one else needs to know."

"Except your brothers," I say bitterly.

"Miller thinks he's funny, but he doesn't mean anything by it. I shouldn't have told him, but I was shocked. I didn't know what to do. He won't tell anyone."

"That's not what it seemed like at the table."

"He won't," Mason says firmly. "He's just jealous."

"Jealous?"

"Yeah. He's attracted to you. I can tell."

I scoff, the very idea that yet another Adonis might find me attractive is too much for me to accept. At least with Mason, I have an artistic connection. Miller doesn't know anything about me.

"And Max."

"What?"

"Max told me that you're smoking hot."

"I have bed-hair and bleary eyes."

"And a lovely just-been-fucked glow." Mason grins, those dimples that set my heart fluttering yesterday having the same overwhelming effect.

"Yeah, just been fucked by their brother. That must make me really appealing."

"You have no idea," Mason says.

"What?"

Mason shrugs and gazes out at the horizon line. "We're triplets. We're used to sharing."

"Sharing?"

That naughty expression that he had when he was flirting with me yesterday returns. He leans in close and the scent of his cologne, sends my head swimming. "Have you ever been shared?"

I'm still not getting what he means. Shared. By what? More than one man?

"I don't cheat," I say. "When I'm with someone, I'm with them."

"That's not what I mean. I mean, shared by men who know about each other…at the same time."

A flush rises up my neck and across my face. Is he serious? Of course I haven't. Who the hell does that?

"No!"

"You don't have to sound so shocked." He smiles. "There are lots of benefits."

"Benefits?"

"Three times the attention. Three times the fun. Three times the pleasure."

"I think one time is enough for me."

"I think you could take more."

The word "take" does funny things to me that I would never have anticipated, but this man really does have some cheek, and also a much-inflated impression of what I'm capable of taking. I'm a one-man woman. Always have been, always will be. Mason by himself is more man than I can comfortably deal with. The sore feeling between my legs is evidence of that. Three Masons, which is what he's effectively taking about, would tear me apart.

They're my stepbrothers, and now he's suggesting all three of them become my lovers.

I thought many things about Mason, but I would never have guessed he'd suggest something like this. The question is, how am I going to respond?

# 12

"I think you drank too much champagne at lunchtime," I say.

"Not enough to wipe the taste of you from my lips," Mason says. "We were good together. Not good…great. Are you telling me you don't want to experience that again?"

"I'm telling you that things aren't as simple as that. Regardless of how good it was, it can't happen again. I told you that, and then you suggested adding your brothers to the mix. What the hell?"

"We can make you feel so good," Mason says. "And I think right now, you need to feel good."

He's making me mad with his presumptions, but they are so on point I could slap him. I don't like being read so easily, and I don't like that all this talk of making me feel good is making me wet. My body is a traitorous thing. If it had its way, I'd be lying spread-eagled on a bed somewhere with three god-like men waiting to pleasure me. Forget my heart, which is aching and my mind, which is screaming to run in the opposite direction.

I've never even thought about group sex before, and now the image of the Banbury brothers and me is burning in my mind.

"I need to just get on with my life," I say. "I don't need complications."

"Life is as complicated as you make it," Mason says. "The offer is there. You can take it whenever you want."

Oh God. Why does he have to say it that way? Now I feel like a kid with a bag full of candy. Temptation like this is as bitter as it is sweet.

"I'm not up for being used," I say.

"Who said anything about using you? It'd be you using us. We'd be at your disposal, Natalie. Just like last night, you'd have to tell us what you want."

"I want you to forget about last night. Pretend it never happened. Tell Miller and Max the same, okay? For all of our sakes." And with that, I turn and storm down the beach. The only way to clear my head from this crazy is to leave Mason and his fantasy ideas behind me.

But it doesn't work.

I walk for an hour until my feet are wrinkled by the ocean, and my face is tender from the sun. By the time I reach the beach house again, I'm exhausted, and I still need to review the shots from yesterday and send them through to the publisher.

I make it to my room without bumping into anyone, shower away the beach, and Mason, emerging with a clearer head. Then I sit at the desk with my laptop and try to process the images of the man who's gotten so far under my skin that I can hardly breathe.

I check off each of the requested shots, finding the best image to match, editing, and labeling so that everything is clear for the client. I try to maintain an impassive attitude, but it's impossible when flashes of Mason fucking me keep coming back with every new image. After three hours, I'm done, and then I feel like I need another shower.

I pull up the images of Mason's paintings on my phone and flick through them slowly. They really are awe inspiring, and I still can't believe that he's holding himself back by not letting anyone see them. I flick through my contacts, finding Beresford's details. We were at college together, and then he went to work in his father's gallery in New York. I'm not sure whether they deal in art like Mason's, but I'm pretty sure he will know someone who'd be interested. You'd have to be blind not to see the skill and originality in his paintings.

It's a strange feeling to send these images without Mason's permission. I know that producing creatively can feel like expressing a part of your soul. It's why I hate that Nate still has my images on his blog. Those are things I made with my skill and my eye for capturing beauty. Am I doing the right thing? I press send because I know that if Beresford's reaction to the images is negative, Mason will never know. If there's a chance I can help Mason move forward, I think the risk that he'll be mad is worth taking.

It's now early evening, and my stomach is rumbling, so I head downstairs to grab a light snack. It's tranquil in the house, which is not what I was expecting.

I bump into the man who served lunch on my way to the kitchen. "Can I help you at all, ma'am?"

"I was going to get something to eat."

"What would you like. I can bring it to you."

"Just something simple. A grilled cheese?"

"That's no problem. And to drink?"

"Just some iced water."

"Would you like it to your room or somewhere else?"

"I'll eat on the deck," I say. I hope that it'll be peaceful out there at this hour. I love the early evening light when the sun is on its way down and everything seems in sharper focus. I have a book on my phone that I can read to kill some time.

As I take a seat at the lovely outdoor table on the deck, everything is exactly as I imagined. No sounds disturb the quiet hush of the waves lapping except the occasional call of birds. It's idyllic. My book is a romance novel that was recommended in one of the magazines I picked up at the airport a few weeks ago. It's all about love in a small town and seems so blissfully simple that I get lost in how easy love can be in someone's imagination.

Real life isn't anything like that, at least not for me. There's always something wrong. Either the men are cheaters like Nate, or into kinky group sex like Mason. A small bemused chuckle leaves my lips as I imagine what Connie would say if she knew.

As though her ears are burning, my phone suddenly switches from Kindle mode to call mode, and Connie's name flashes across the screen.

"There you are," she says as though she's been trying to get hold of me all day.

"Here I am," I say.

"I was expecting you to call me with an update yesterday, but I got the shots before I got the update."

"What do you think?"

"Fucking amazing, but I knew they would be."

Smiling broadly, I rest my head in my hand, prepared for a long chat. No phone call with Connie is ever short.

"That's good. I was really nervous."

"I'm not surprised. I think I would have passed out if I had to take images of that sexy man. How did you keep your cool?"

"I didn't," I say. "I was a sweaty mess for most of the day."

She snorts with laughter. "That's my girl. So what was he like?"

"Really professional."

"Oh yeah." There's a pause on the phone, and I know Connie well enough that she has her insightful expression on right now that involves her narrowing her eyes and twisting her pursed lips to one side. There are definite pros and cons to having a friend who has known you forever. Pros involve all the funny memories you can reminisce about and how they know how you're going to be feeling before you know yourself. Cons involve them guessing your secrets just by your words and tone, and that's what Connie's trying to do right now.

"You fucked him," she says with a gasp.

"Oh, please."

"Don't 'oh please' me Natalie, you dawg. You better be about to share all the details with me, or I won't tell you what I was calling to tell you, and believe me, you want me to tell you."

"I just don't understand how you guess this stuff. Either you have a private investigator reporting back on all my movements, or you're some kind of psychic. Even I wouldn't have guessed that I'd do what I did. I nearly didn't."

"It's the rebound fuck," Connie says definitely. "We all do it. When we've been burned, we look for the nearest dick and ride away our sorrows."

"Lovely imagery," I laugh.

"Are you telling me that isn't what happened?"

I run my hands over my face, the blush that has sprung to my cheeks embarrassing, even though she can't see it. "Among other things," I say.

"Well, now we're getting somewhere. Multiple positions, eh. Mason must have been as good as he looked."

"He was better," I say with a sigh.

"Shit…that makes it harder."

"Harder, how?"

"Well, the rebound fuck is great if it's poor to average. You get the previous asshole out of your system, but you're not tempted to jump into another relationship because the sex isn't good enough…but with you…"

"There's not going to be a relationship."

"Why? Is he dumb?"

"No…he's an amazing artist."

"Ohhh…things in common too…very dangerous ground."

It's at that moment that my grilled cheese sandwich appears, carried on a large tray with a silver dome atop. It's like the finest five-star service. There's a slice of lime in my iced water and a straw; little things that highlight the difference between my life here and my old life with Mom.

"Let me know if you require anything else," the man says as he lifts the dome with a flourish.

"Wow." It looks like the best grilled-cheese ever.

"What are you wowing about?" Connie asks.

"A grilled-cheese sandwich," I laugh.

"You're interrupting our discussion about sex with a hot model to talk about comfort food. Ah…you're eating comfort food."

"I'm…yeah, I guess I am."

"Tell me details, please. Take pity on your poor friend, who has been relationshipless for way too long. There are cobwebs between my thighs, Natalie. Seriously."

"It was…he made me ask for whatever I wanted. I had to be in charge."

"So he's a sub?" Connie's voice has gone from excited to intrigued.

"No…he…I guess I don't really understand it. I think he wanted me to be sure of each step we took."

"Mmmm…interesting. He sounds…intuitive. Not a typical male trait."

"I know. But anyway, it doesn't matter that it was the best sex I ever had because I got home this morning and found him having lunch here. He's Conrad's son. I mean, what are the odds."

"WHATTTT?"

"I know, right? Even if I was in a place to start something with him, which I'm not, it's not going to happen now!"

"Why the hell not? You know he's from a great family. You'll be under the same roof, so plenty of opportunities. It could be the perfect way to get over Nasty Nate."

"When did you start calling him that?"

"When you started dating him," Connie replies abruptly. Is she serious?

"Why didn't you tell me you didn't like him?"

"Because you did, and I didn't want to burst your bubble. I mean, what do I know? I'm hardly the writer of the successful relationships manual. I thought maybe I was my usual judgmental bitch self and that you saw something in him that I didn't."

"I think you saw the truth. You should trust your instincts more and tell me if you feel like that in the future, okay? I know it might be hard for me to hear, but I'll never hold it against you. I know you have my best interests at heart."

"Okay, deal. And what about Mason? What do you think of him?"

"I thought he was a really good guy. The kind of guy that I'd have seriously considered a second date and more with."

"There sounds like there's a big but."

"There is. The stepbrother thing is weird, but he started talking about how he'd want to share me with his two brothers."

I hear a choking sound on the other end of the phone that tells me I've done the unthinkable and shocked Connie. This is a moment to commit to memory.

"And this is a 'but' why exactly?"

"Err, did you not hear what I said?" I take a second big bite of my sandwich and chew hurriedly. I'm hungry, but I want to hear what Connie has to say and be able to respond without sandwich flying out of my mouth.

"I did…and I am dying that I'm not you right now. You've just been offered my fantasy on a plate, and you are talking about it like it's something you need to be running away from."

I take a sip of my drink, shake my head. "Are you serious? You fantasize about that?"

"And you don't. Oh my God. Just imagine it. One man who looks like that is heaven-sent. Three…well you must have been a saint in a past life. I'm so seriously jealous of you I'm developing the Hulk's complexion."

I laugh, filled with disbelief at my crazy friend. Even after all these years, I'm still finding out weird and wonderful things about her. "One man is hard enough to deal with. Forget three. I'd be a wreck."

"Yeah, and for all the right reasons. I want you to think about yourself in sixty years. You're an old woman looking back on her youth. Do you think you'll look back and regret going ahead with Mason's suggestion, or do you think you'll regret saying no?"

Trust Connie to bring perspective into this. The decisions we make feel huge when they're imminent, but time and hindsight change who we are and how we see things. Will I regret never knowing what it would be like? It's exactly the reason I changed my mind last night and slept with Mason.

"I just don't think I can do it," I say. "I'm just not that confident."

"Well, you should be. You're an awesome person. Beautiful inside and out. Any man would be lucky to have you…in any capacity."

"Awww…thanks hon." I wish my bestie was next to me so I could hug her for her kindness. "But I mean, I don't think I'd know how to ask for what I want from three men, and that would be what I needed to do."

"I want you to read a novel tonight…I'll send you the link. It might help you see things a little differently."

"A novel?"

"Yeah. It's about a similar situation. A girl who doesn't know whether to go through with something like this."

"A romance novel."

"Exactly."

"I don't see how that will help me, but I could do with some escapism."

"And I'm going to send you details for the wrap-up shoot tomorrow. Now that the author has seen the images, she has a few more shots for promotional material. It looks like you'll get to spend another day in Mason's stimulating company."

"I…I don't think that's a good idea." How the hell am I going to go through more time with Mason in a professional way after what happened between us?

"Well, they're offering a nice bonus to complete the job. I think you'd be mad to turn it down…and it wouldn't look good."

Connie's right. If I walk away before the client is completely happy, that will leave them scrambling to find someone who can match my style on the rest of the shots. It's a huge inconvenience and could mean that all the shots need redoing.

"I guess I'll have to find a way through it," I say, cringing.

"I guess you will. Such a hardship," Connie says in a voice dripping with sarcasm.

Tomorrow will bring a whole new level of complication, but I have to admit that even though the shoot is going to be awkward, I'm kind of excited at the prospect.

# 13

I sleep very restlessly. My dreams are infiltrated by a shadowy man who commands my body so completely that I'm paralyzed and defenseless while he takes what he wants. When my alarm goes off, I find myself as aroused as I am during real sex. My heart is racing, too, as though everything that happened in my subconscious was experienced as reality by my body.

It's been a long time since I brought myself to orgasm, but I slide my hand into my panties and rub my clit until my back is bowed and my thighs clenching with the release. It's Mason who's in my mind when it happens, and that makes the prospect of seeing him in a couple of hours that much harder.

I choose my clothes carefully, avoiding my usual voluminous blouses and pants in favor of a floral maxi dress with a halter neck that ties prettily at my nape. Conrad's driver is available to take me downtown, and this time my journey is filled with excited anticipation. What will Mason be like today? Will he be flirty, or will he maintain his distance? Did I put him off entirely with my frosty response yesterday, or will he disregard my arguments and continue to push for more?

Andre is there to show me to the studio area, and unlike last time, Mason has arrived before me. He's lounging in an armchair, his legs splayed wide and attention fixed on his phone. When he hears my sandals' sound on the polished concrete floor, his gaze fixes on me, and he smiles broadly. Instead of being cool and composed, I blush from my décolletage to my hairline, becoming a giant tomato in a flounce of floral. Ridiculous. I really need to get a life.

"So, more shots," Mason says.

Placing my camera equipment down on the table, I begin to unload everything in preparation. "They liked the other shots so much that they wanted to commission more."

"That's good for me. More work equals more money."

"Exactly," I say.

"Where will you want me first?"

I glance over the outline for the shoot and blush again. Most of today's work is going to involve Mason being shirtless through to naked. There aren't any shots where his cock will be in view, but there are some where he'll be required to use a sheet or his hand to conceal himself. Our previous intimacy makes shots these problematic. So problematic.

"Here's the outline," I say. "You can keep this copy to refer to." I reach out and hand it to Mason, who is now standing in front of my work station.

"That's quite a set-up you have there," he says.

"Just the same as before." I shrug, looking over my precious equipment. It's more than my livelihood. Taking beautiful photographs has become such a fundamental part of who I am that my camera feels like an extension of my body. An extension of my body that will, in a moment, capture the beauty of Mason's.

He smiles, his pretty blue eyes filled with warmth, and I'm filled with the same butterflies as I was when I first met him. "I'll get ready," he says, taking the outline and heading behind the screen.

I finish my preparations as Mason tugs on the form-fitting jeans and boots required for this shoot. The author has asked for shots of him leaning up against the brick wall with one foot resting against it, and his thumbs hooked in his belt. She also wants one where he's smoking in the same position. I don't like the idea of Mason infecting his lungs with smoke for a photograph, but I guess he's used to giving his body over to whatever is required of him for the job.

I take a few test shots, adjusting the lighting as I go, trying to get everything as perfect as I can before Mason is in front of me and I have to deal with looking at him.

It's tougher than I thought it would be.

My body has too much memory. The push of his huge cock into my…

"You're blushing," Mason says, standing closer than I realized, and I jump and flush even more.

"It's hot in here," I say, even though it isn't. If anything, it's a little on the cool side. "The first shot is against the wall. Can you stand with your back against that brickwork and your left foot up?"

Mason takes his position, the muscles across his bare chest rippling with every movement. I remember how it felt to rest my palms on his skin as he worked to bring me pleasure. Fuck, it felt good, but there's no touching now.

Not ever again. I'm determined not to exchange too many words with him today. I'm definitely not going to get drawn into talking about our night together. That would just be mortifying.

"Lift your foot just a little higher." He does as I ask, those deep blue eyes sliding over me as I work. "That's it. And hook your right thumb into your jeans pocket…perfect. I'll take a few shots head-on and then a few in profile with you gazing out of the window."

Mason nods, and I snap away, shutter clicking like paparazzi at a film premiere. I'm going to take double the number of shots I usually take today so that I capture everything. There's no way I'm putting myself through another day of this torture.

"That's it. Now turn. Keep your neck straight…perfect."

As soon as his eyes are turned from mine, I feel my body relax. Capturing his profile is so much easier – the perfect strong slant of his nose and jut of his stubbly chin. His long eyelashes give his masculine form the extra softness that makes something in my chest ache, even at this distance.

It's the same when I see paintings that touch my soul – the same when I hear a melody that reaches deep inside. Beauty has always had a very physical effect on me, and Mason has that beauty.

"Undo your belt and the buttons on your jeans." Even as I give these professional instructions, I remember those that I gave Mason in the hotel room. He concentrates, a small frown appearing between his brow. He's wearing plain black underwear that dips low, revealing the perfect undulations of his abs. I licked across there, tasting the saltiness of his skin after the second time we fucked. I ran my fingers over that stomach and felt the life inside him.

I snap away, the images I'm creating beautiful but lacking the vitality and strength of the real man. I take a step back in frustration, wanting more, and needing more.

"Can you rub some of this into your skin?" I say, grasping the bottle of oil that has been provided for the shoot. "Not too much."

Again, he does as I ask, and the thrill affects me more than it should. As his skin begins to glisten, I adjust the lighting again. Mason rests the bottle out of the shot and smooths his palms over his chest and abs, spreading the oil into his skin a little more. "Good?"

"Very good." Oh God, that sounded wrong. It sounded flirtatious. It sounded sexual, and that's probably because that's exactly how I feel.

Mason's mouth quirks on one side with the briefest glimmer of a smile. He takes position again, and I snap a test shot, pondering on whether it's enough. There's something wrong with his hair today. It's too preened.

"Can I…" I place my camera down and move closer to him. "It's your hair."

He nods, but even with his permission, this feels difficult. I'm close enough to know that he's wearing a different scent today. Close enough to feel a buzz across my skin from his proximity. I gently run my fingers through his thick hair so that it's looser and a little messier. Like this, he looks more like the bad boy the client wants. Hair disrupted by the fingers of the women who can't resist him. That couldn't be more true.

I snap away, asking Mason to move to fulfill all the requirements of the brief, except the final part of the shoot. He needs to lose the rest of his clothes for that, and I think I might lose my mind.

"Okay," I say and then clear my throat because it comes out huskily. "We just have the last part to complete now."

Mason nods. "You want me to lose the clothes?"

Why the hell does he have to ask me that? It's as though he wants to see me squirm.

"Yep. That's what the client wants."

That flicker of a smile is there again, his eyes as bright as the ocean behind Conrad's beach house. "The client. Of course."

He saunters behind the screen, and I'm left listening to the tantalizing rustle of him removing the last barrier between him and my sanity. My pussy squeezes involuntarily, the thought of his nakedness too much to face without effect. I busy myself, viewing images on the larger screen, forcing myself to inhale deeply.

Mason appears with his hand concealing his cock as much as it possibly can, and he clears his throat. "On the bed?"

"Yeah. There's a loose sheet for you to pull through your legs to conceal…" I pause, the words not forming in my brain.

"My cock," he says abruptly, and I flinch.

"Exactly."

I don't watch as he takes a seat on the edge of the bed and swings his legs up. I don't watch as he gathers the pure white cotton sheet to cover the most sinful, perfect, amazing cock that I've ever had the privilege to encounter. I lick my lips and then flinch again, realizing that my body is giving too much away about the arousal I'm feeling.

"Is this good?" I glance up, finding Mason tangled perfectly in the sheets as though he's just finished blowing some lucky girl's mind and is relaxing in his own glory. Oh God, I don't think I can do this. I really don't.

I pick up the armor of my camera to view the shot in safety, without my flushing face in full view. I chew my bottom lip, concentrating on what is going to make this image absolutely mind-blowing.

Less sheet.

I'm going to need to adjust the fabric and ask Mason to adjust himself to make his cock a little more tantalizingly obvious in the image. It's what the client wants, after all.

"One second." Approaching the bed, I rest the camera on the end. "Can you just…" My mouth dries on the next words.

"You want me to move my cock?"

"Bring it upwards, so it's just to the left of your navel and hold it there. I'll move the sheet."

I make the mistake of looking into Mason's eyes at exactly that moment and see the swell of his pupils that darken his eyes until his gaze is dripping with sex. Leaning over him like this, my cleavage is more obvious. Does he notice? Do I want him to?

Taking hold of the fabric, I pull it down enough so that it will only just keep Mason modest. I guess it helps that I know exactly what he looks like beneath this scrap of fabric and the memory is measurable in my mind. I want his perfectly muscular thigh more on show, especially the part between his legs, which somehow seems more explicit. My fingers itch to trail across that sensitive area and see Mason shiver. I know he would. But I can't.

"Okay, take your hand away slowly."

Things move around a little but not enough to disrupt the effect of the shot. The slight shift of his cock under the sheets disrupts me between my legs, though.

"Perfect," I say through a gulp.

I step back quickly, tangling my feet in the long fabric of my skirt and stumbling before I stabilize myself. "Stupid dress," I mutter, grabbing my camera and flushing with embarrassment.

"It looks pretty good to me," Mason says.

It's the longest hour of my life. With every new shot, I have to face Mason in ever more explicit ways. The amazing curve of his ass and V of his back makes me want to fall to my knees and worship him. I don't know what I've done to deserve this, but it must be something terrible. Really bad because this whole day has been painful, and I'm a sweaty, flustered, wet-and-achy-between-my-legs mess. Oh, and Mason is as cool as a cucumber.

"I think we're done," I say, wanting to flop into the chair and fan myself for at least an hour.

Mason nods, his hand cupping between his legs. "Great."

He saunters back to the screen, and I get to commit the sexiest walk of all time to memory, and I start to see what Connie was talking about yesterday. Today has been so hard. Mason is almost impossible to resist, but I know I'm going to look back on this as one of the best days of my life. Imagine what memories of Mason and his brothers would be like. Hot as hell. Fuel to heat even my coldest and darkest of days.

I begin to pack everything while Mason gets dressed. I'm going to do what I did yesterday and review the shots in detail in the privacy of my room. When I'm done, Mason emerges back in his street clothes, hair still messy from my fingers, and he takes my breath away. Maybe he catches the way that my chest hitches, or maybe I'm still red across my chest from arousal. Maybe he just has a sixth sense, or maybe he's just an opportunist who's prepared to push his luck, even when he's been turned down once already.

"Wanna get a hotel room and work off all of the sexual tension?" he says, shrugging as though he's offering to buy me a coffee rather than fuck me senseless.

And I should say no. I should tell him to take a running jump off a cliff, but I don't.

I shrug, too, like the whole thing was inevitable from the moment I walked in this morning, and he reaches for the strap of my camera bag, happy to provide me with a carrier service for that too.

Am I stupid? Probably. Do I care?

At this point, not at all!

# 14

There's a hotel around the corner from the warehouse, and we're silent for most of the way. Instead of conversation, the air between us vibrates with sexual tension, the anticipation of what's going to happen next almost too much for me to bear.

Like last time, Mason pays for the room and leads me to the elevator, smiling enigmatically. Maybe he's different this time because we've been here before. Or it could be because I was so against the idea of repeating what we did. Whatever it is, I guess it doesn't matter.

We're back here for one reason and one reason only; to scratch each other's itch.

If he wants me to tell him what to do, I'm not going to have any problem today. Gone is the shy Natalie from our first night. He's going to give me what I want, exactly the way I want it. He's the one who's worked me into this frenzy, and he's going to work me out of it.

Like last time, he opens the door to the room and rests my heavy bag on the desk. It's a different room, fancier than the last one but I don't care. He could have taken me to a seedy motel, and it wouldn't have mattered as long as it had a bed and clean sheets.

I don't wait around, untying the neck of my dress and pulling it down. My halter-neck bra is baby blue lace, and I even wore the matching panties, which have blue ribbon ties at each side. I kick the dress off, and my shoes, loving the way Mason folds in his lips to wet them in anticipation.

"Tell me what you want," he says.

"I want you to fuck me the way you want. I want to know exactly what you'd do to me if you could control it all."

"Fuck," he mutters, pulling the back of his shirt and practically tearing it away from his body. It's flung across the room while he toes off his shoes and socks, and throws his jeans to the floor. He stalks across the room with no patience for the flirtatious back and forth, no restraint for the game. Grabbing me behind the thighs, he picks me up with force, pressing me against the wall, his mouth on mine with a ferocity that makes my heart pound. So this is what Mason is like when he's given free rein. A caged animal finally freed.

He holds me with one hand and the weight of his body, using his other palm to squeeze my breast and then force my bra upward so I'm bared to him. The pinch of his fingers on my nipple is perfect pleasure-pain, and I gasp against his lips, which makes him smile.

There's something more devilish about Mason tonight that I can't put my finger on. It's in the way he grinds against my pussy, teasing but then stopping just as I throw my head back, relishing in the sensations. It's there in the nips he gives my throat and the way he grips my ass just a little bit too tight.

And I respond with a little more force than usual, digging my short nails into his shoulders as I hang on for dear life.

Then he's tossing me on the bed with as much care as he took when he flung his shirt, and pinning me down while he looks me over.

"You really are fucking sexy," he says roughly. "The sexiest woman I've seen in a very long time." I blink up at him, not sure how to respond. I've never been good at taking compliments. To be honest, I've not received many as forcefully projected as that one. "And I think you're sexier because you don't even know it."

He pulls at the ribbon on the left of my panties and trails the material to one side, revealing the soft blonde hair at the apex of my thighs. He hisses as he runs one thick finger down the slick seam of my pussy, parting it with an urgency that has me gasping.

I'm expecting him to put his mouth between my legs the way he did before, but he doesn't. Instead, he flips me onto my belly, tugging me under my waist until I'm on all fours, then he positions himself behind me, stroking the curve of my ass with two rough palms. "I like you like this. Ready and waiting for me."

And I am. Oh, I am. Waiting with bated breath for that amazing feeling of his cock forcing its way inside me. "Now," I tell him, the anticipation too much.

"No," he says. Then I feel him moving behind me, the bed dipping as he lies on his back. "Sit on my face, baby. Let me taste you.

Oh…he's on his back, his face beneath me, gazing up at my splayed pussy. There's no waiting for my acquiescence. He just roughly tugs me by the hips until my clit is poised above his mouth, and then he's sucking at me hungrily, tongue flicking with the perfect amount of pressure. It feels so good…so damn amazing that my hips move, grinding me harder onto his filthy mouth. He grunts, fingers pressing deep into my flesh, and I hear the slick sound of him stroking himself at the same time. I wish I could see what that was like, and I guess that there's a way that I can.

"I want to suck you," I say, and Mason stops suddenly.

"Turn around," he orders. I guess the rules of the game aren't as straightforward as before. Maybe because this is our second time, and I'm telling him what I want more freely. I do as he asks, and he tugs my pussy to his mouth, the different angle changing everything. I flop forward, resting on one arm, using the other to take over from Mason. I stroke his hot, heavy cock and flick my tongue out to lick the tip. His hips jerk, which makes me smile. For such a big man, he's certainly very sensitive when it comes to teasing. I maintain the pumps of my hand, licking out every so often until Mason's hips rise up, and his cock bumps into my lips.

"Suck it," he says. "Or I won't let you come."

Shit, that's hot as hell. I'm so close that I almost do it at the sound of his voice. I sink down, taking his cock as deep as I can, the taste of him filling my senses until my head is spinning. I don't care about my breathing becoming ragged or how messy my face is getting. I don't care when Mason slaps my ass and pushes more fingers inside me than I know what to do with. I'm a moaning, frantic cock-sucking mess, pushed to my absolute limits, and it's the most freeing experience of my life.

And just as I'm about to come all over his face, he stops, pushing me roughly onto my back.

I'm disoriented when he looms over me, flushed face and panting, lips slick from my pussy. I'm not expecting him to find my entrance and push inside me in one deep and punishing thrust. I'm certainly not prepared to come violently at that moment, and it's like a sweeping wave of relief hits me right in the face, forcing my back to arch and my mouth to open, sending stars swimming across my vision.

"Fuck," he mutters, my pussy bearing down on him like a vice. He pumps through it though; eyes fixed on my face as I come down from the stratosphere.

He fucks me as though his life depends on it. Like I'm the only woman in the world, and it's his mission to claim me for the human race's future. I relish everything because this is the last time.

I have to tell him when all this is done. One of us has to be strong, or everything's going to be ruined.

When he comes, it's like an exorcism, and he doesn't stop fucking into me through it all, filling me with the hot, slick cum that I held onto for so long last time.

And after, he kisses me tenderly. He tells me I'm amazing and beautiful and sexy. He strokes my face and gazes at me with satisfaction resting lazily in his expression.

"That was fucking phenomenal," he says with a bubble of disbelieving laughter.

"It was," I say, starting to think about what comes next. I'm not going to fall asleep again only to wake up alone, and I'm not going to lie here pretending that this is more than it is, but just as I'm about to make an excuse to get up and dressed, he runs his hand over my stomach until it rests over my breast.

"He was right about you."

I blink, not understanding. "Who was?"

"Mason," he says.

And just like that, my world spins out of control.

# 15

I jerk backward. "What?"

"Mason. He told me you were amazing, and he was right. What made you change your mind?"

"Change my mind?" My voice comes out like a high-pitched squeak with the realization that I just had sex with a man I thought was someone else.

"Yeah. Mason said that you weren't into the idea."

"Idea?" Oh my God, this is Miller. It can't be Max because he doesn't have any tattoos.

This is Miller!

"He said you didn't want to get involved with us. Are you okay?"

I guess that Miller must have noticed that I'm frozen rigid with shock. I guess the fact that I'm tugging the sheet over my naked body must seem a little odd after I just sat on his face.

I just sat on Miller's face.

What have I done?

"You're not Mason," I stutter, and it's Miller's turn to jerk backward.

"Mason?" He closes his eyes and draws in a long breath. "You thought I was Mason."

"Err…of course I thought you were Mason. You came to the shoot today. You…you look just like him. You pretended to be him."

"No." Miller pushes himself up and leans back against the headboard. "I didn't pretend to be him. Did you not read the client documents? It listed me as the model for today. Mason was booked out of town."

"No, I didn't."

"And you thought I was him?" Miller folds his arms, his shoulders tight and raised.

"Yes." I run my hand over my face, the realization that it was my assumptions that got us into this mess is totally mortifying. "I'm sorry."

Miller snorts. "Sorry. You don't need to be sorry. I just had the best sex I've had for months because of a case of mistaken identity. Are you okay, though?"

"I don't know," I say. "This is…well, it's weird."

"Well, it's not the first time someone's been confused between us, but it's the first that I've gotten laid because of it."

Oh, my goodness. This is so embarrassing that I don't even know what to do with myself. I don't want to make Miller feel bad by dashing away now I know he's not his brother, but I'm totally thrown. I don't know what to do or how to act.

"Hey." Miller rests his hand on my shoulder. It's big and strong and comforting, placed gently to give me some reassurance. "Natalie, I know you must be feeling weird about this. I just…I guess I should be sorry."

"What for? You didn't do anything. It was me."

"Maybe we should have both been a little more verbal today before falling into bed with each other." Miller cocks his head to one side, smiling his filthy smile that I can now see is very different from his brother's. "But then we wouldn't have had all this fun."

I snort, thinking about how different today was to my time with Mason. They might be triplets, but they're not identical in every way. Is that what it would be like to be with all of them? I started the novel that Connie recommended last night, and the author spoke about how being with more than one man could mean finding complementary characteristics among the group. If you need a man to be gentle and kind, you'll have one. Need one to be rough and demanding, and you have it on tap. It's selfish for sure because how does one woman truly satisfy more than one man. I couldn't ever be enough for them.

"Fun is dangerous," I say, rolling onto my back and staring at the perfectly smooth, white ceiling. If only life could be as simple.

"Fun is what makes the world turn," Miller says.

"I just…" I pause, the words for what to say next disappearing in my mouth.

"You feel like this was a mistake?"

"I feel like everything I do is a mistake."

"I get that," Miller says. His hand strokes the hair back from my face in a gesture that feels too tender for where and who we are. "But don't you think that it's all a matter of perspective?"

"What do you mean?"

"Just that you can see things as mistakes, or as stepping stone on the journey of life. We can't always do the right thing…being human, we get to go wrong and then to learn."

"I don't seem to be that good at learning." I sigh, the deep-down disappointment in the bad decisions I've been making lately sitting like a weight on my chest.

"I think you sound like you're hard on yourself. Like today, you can think of this as a big mistake. You can kick yourself for making assumptions, for not asking the right questions, or you could see it as something good that happened. We got to experience something pretty damned amazing. I mean…fuck." Miller shakes his head. "I really want to do that again."

"Again?"

"Don't you?"

My traitorous clit tingles at the thought. Mistake or amazing? Miller says it's all about perspective, and I guess he's right. I can walk away from this room kicking myself, or smiling. I can make memories for my eighty-year-old self to smile about, or I can bury shameful secrets. Is it that easy to flip your mind around to decide which perspective to take?

"What do you say, Natalie? Ready to see how great your mistake can be?" He climbs over me, knees straddling my hips, long, thick cock hard and ready to take me to places that I really want to go to.

Stepping stones on the journey of life.

I like his perspective.

When he kisses me, I forget why I ever thought this was a bad idea.

# 16

"What will you tell Mason?" I ask Miller when the night has ebbed into the early morning, and our sweat has finally cooled.

"The truth," he says. "We don't keep secrets, and we don't lie to each other. It's the way it's always been."

"Will he be mad?" The idea that there won't be jealousy between them still doesn't ring true to me.

"No. He'll be happy, for you especially."

"Why for me?" Miller draws me closer to him, my back pressing deeper into the nook of his chest as he spoons me.

"Because he…he feels something about you. Something that he wants to free."

"What do you mean?"

"He told me about the game he made you play. He told me that he pushed you to ask for what you wanted…that he knew that wasn't a natural part of who you are right now."

“It isn’t,” I say. “I don’t think it ever has been.”

Miller kisses the back of my head. “We’re not born with everything we need to deal with life,” he says. “Sometimes, we have to recognize that and find ways to learn and to adapt.”

“You and Mason. You’re very perceptive.”

“Mason sees the world for what it is. He sees through pretense to the truth of people. I think it’s because he’s an artist. His eyes take things apart so that he can put them back together again in his own way.”

“And you?”

I can feel Miller’s smile against my scalp. “I’m a psychologist.”

Turning in his arms, I see the man whose taste is still fresh in my mouth in a new light. “You are?”

He nods. “I have my own practice.”

“Well, that explains a lot.”

Miller shrugs. “I don’t like to tell people. I think they immediately start to think that I’m analyzing them.”

“And aren’t you?”

He shrugs. “I guess it’s hard to turn off that part of my brain. Like Mason will see potential paintings he could do everywhere he goes, and Max sees the potential for trouble before it’s happened, I see people.”

“Max?”

“He’s head of security for a hotel and casino.”

“Ah.” I can imagine Max dressed up in a black suit with an earpiece and gun strapped under his jacket. He has that strong, capable air about him that would inspire confidence, even in the most challenging situations.

"It can make relationships difficult," Miller says.

"I can understand that. It's hard enough trying to work yourself out on a daily basis, let alone having someone that you love doing it." Miller sighs, and I lean in to kiss his lips, realizing after I've spoken that this is exactly his fear. "But maybe when it's someone you love, it won't be so hard to hear. I think it could be helpful to me to be with someone who can untangle my thoughts every so often."

"You don't have to say that to make me feel better."

I smile, seeing him seeing me. "You think I'm a people pleaser."

He tucks my hair behind my ear and kisses my forehead in a way that makes me melt. "I think you're a very kind person who expects less for herself than she gives to others."

"And you, Miller Banbury. What are you?"

He smirks, rolling onto his back and resting his arm across his forehead. Before we started this conversation, I wouldn't have thought anything of it, but now I see the defensiveness in his body language and the fact he put distance between himself and the question. Miller is a man who likes to understand people, but he has definite barriers to others doing the same with him.

"I'm a man who needs to use the bathroom."

He swings his legs off the side of the bed and saunters around the room with no hint of concern for his nakedness. I mean, if I looked like him, I wouldn't have any concern either. In fact, I'm pretty happy he's content to give me a show that most women would give their life-savings for. When he closes the door, I chuckle gently to myself.

Mistake.

I can't believe I was thinking that way about something so fantastic. Maybe Miller's right. Maybe it is all about perspective.

And my perspective on Miller's ass is definitely not something I'm planning to regret.

# 17

This time I make sure that I message Mom to let her know that I'm staying with a friend so that when I fall asleep tucked into Miller's arms, I don't have to worry about what I'm going to have to face at home in a few hours.

Part of me wonders whether Miller will be there when I wake, but part of me doesn't care. This is what it is. A stepping stone on my journey. An experience that I will always remember as a positive one. Miller is a great guy, filled with insight and empathy. He's made me feel good about my body and good about myself. He's showed me a new way of thinking that has lifted the pressure I've felt for so much of my life. Who knows how long this will last, but for now, I'm languishing in peace and contentment.

In the morning, Miller is still there, sleeping curled on his side facing me so that I have time to really study him. There's a scar on his left cheek that I didn't notice before – a scar that Mason doesn't have, an experience that separates them.

When he wakes, he tugs me on top of him, kissing me with no care for our morning breath and sliding me onto his waiting cock, and I marvel at how easy it is between us after such a short amount of time together.

His car is parked in an underground garage, and he drives us both back to the beach house, unwilling to listen to my protestations that people will talk. "Who's going to talk?" he says. "I'm giving you a ride, that's all. No one can tell where I've had my mouth and cock."

My cheeks heat at the mental images his words bring back, but he's right. There's no one at the house when we get back, and I head to my room to go through the images. By the time I'm done, it's lunchtime, and I'm ravenous. I tell John, the man who seems to appear whenever I need anything, that I'd like to take my lunch down to the beach. It's the weekend, and I want to get some sun and finish reading the book Connie recommended.

John appears with a cooler filled with delicious-looking treats. I would have made myself a sandwich at home, but here I get to feast on freshly made sushi and soft-berry yogurt dessert that is so yummy, I scrape the bowl until it's almost clean. The sun is shining, and the birds are singing. As the waves lap at the shore, I breathe deeply and then shake my head because it's baffling to me that I could feel so content. I've just had sex with two of my stepbrothers with no idea how they feel about repeating the fun. It's the most open experience I've ever had, and rather than feeling out of control, I actually feel free. Free to ask for what I want. Free to be me.

"There you are."

I look up to see Mason, Miller, and Max dressed in board-shorts and sliders, towels tossed over their shoulders, and what a sight it is. I lower my kindle, the romance novel immediately forgotten.

"It's a day for the beach," I say, watching each of them look me over, my tiny swimwear drawing their attention.

Max runs his hand through his hair, lifting his sunglasses. "Mind if we join you?"

"Of course not. It's your dad's beach. You've got more right to be here than I do."

He shrugs. "This is your home…I meant are we disturbing your reading?"

"The book can wait."

Mason and Miller toss their stuff onto the loungers to my right and Max tosses his onto the lounger to my left, and here I am in the middle of my triplet stepbrothers. Just where Mason wants me to be.

"No work today?"

"I'm on shift tonight," Max says. "These reprobates have the weekend free."

"Yeah, for a change," Miller says.

"I guess listening to other people's problems for a living must be really draining."

Max flops onto his neatly arranged towel and brushes all the sand off his feet before lifting them. Very meticulous.

"More draining than walking around like an extra from Men in Black," Miller laughs.

"Definitely more draining than painting nude women and prancing around half-naked," Max says.

Mason shrugs, shooting me a panty-melting grin that tells me he has no issues with me fucking his brother last night. "The prancing is easier than the painting, but the subject-matter that I get to paint definitely has its benefits."

“So, do you swim?” Max asks.

“Yeah, but I'm better in the pool than the sea. I hate it when the salty water goes up my nose. You guys must be really good at swimming in the ocean.”

“Yeah. Dad paid for us to have lessons out here. He wanted to make sure we could look after ourselves.”

“That's a really great idea.”

“You know, I think you need to put some more cream on,” Max says. “You're starting to get a little red on your shoulders.” With no concern for his sand-less feet, he stands and grabs my lotion from the low table between us and tells me to lean forward.

I might not be great at reading people, but this is definitely less about my shoulders and more about him getting his hands on me. He's the only brother who hasn't had my legs wrapped around him, and as he strokes cream into my skin with slow, sensuous strokes, I definitely sense that it's something he intends to change.

Does it sound weird that now I've had two, the third doesn't seem like so much of an issue?

Connie would be squealing if I said that out loud. She'd be telling me to drag Max into the sea for some underwater fun. A moan escapes my lips, part elicited by Max's strong hands that have no more cream to rub but are still kneading, and part by my fantasy. I've never had sex in water and certainly not in public. Not that this is really public. This house is on substantial grounds, and the next property is way down the shore. Unless someone has a telescope trained on us, they wouldn't be able to see a thing. Maybe the staff at the house would, but I'm pretty sure they signed non-disclosure agreements with their contracts. That's the way of the rich.

I glance down, finding my nipples are hard beneath my floral suit. Maybe it's like muscle memory. Whenever a Banbury brother touches me now, I'll have a sexual response. That's not so terrible right now, but in front of our parents, it would be mortifying.

Ugh.

I push that thought to the back of my mind. We're all grown, and this is just about fun. It's just about scratching an itch for them and about taking another footstep on a path of self-discovery and fulfillment for me. How far can I push past my own inhibitions without any kind of self-doubt or hatred?

"Wanna play paddle ball?" Miller asks Mason.

"Sure."

Miller pulls the bats and a small white rubber ball from his bag and shoots me a grin before jogging down to the shoreline with his brother. Something about that grin has me suspicious that this is a set-up for me to get to know Max, and if that's the case, this is definitely moving into the realms that Mason talked about.

Sex with Mason and Miller separately pushed my boundaries. Sex with Max alone would be a step even further. Sex with all of them at the same time – the kind of sex described in Connie's recommended book – has me flushing from the soles of my feet to the roots of my hair.

I think that's what they want, though. For what reason, I'm not sure, outside of the kink factor. Maybe they enjoy watching someone who looks just like them fucking; a weird egotistical impulse like fucking next to a mirror. Maybe they just enjoy watching in the same way as people get off on porn. Maybe it's something else entirely.

Is it linked to them being triplets? Do they feel like something is missing when they're separate from their brothers? Is sharing one girl about family unity? If so, banging their stepsister must be the ultimate.

I glance at Max, conscious that I've been lost in my own thoughts for a while, and we've been sitting in silence as a result.

He smiles in a slow, lazy way, revealing just one dimple, and it's shocking to me to notice such a difference between Max and his brothers. "Your cheeks are flushed."

I touch my face, finding it hot. "The sun is very strong."

"And you're thinking about sex." Opening my mouth to protest, he puts up a hand to stop me. "It's okay, of course. I am too."

"You are?"

He shrugs. "My brothers have painted quite a picture of you, Natalie, and all those images are swimming around in my head."

"Mason told me you share everything."

"We like to," Max says. "But the chance to share some things doesn't always present itself."

"I can imagine."

He puts his hands behind his head, watching his brothers, who are having some kind of competitive match. "Not many people understand us."

"I think that's a universal problem for most of us in life. It's why so many people suffer from depression, and so many relationships break down."

Max nods. "Well, Miller will know more about that kind of thing."

"He's already set me on the path to self-discovery."

“Yeah, that's his thing. He could do with spending a little more time discovering himself, though.”

“What do you mean?”

Max shrugs. “It's not really my place to talk about my brothers that way. I guess when you get to know us more, you'll see all our scars and flaws.”

“Aren't they what makes us beautiful?” I ask.

We're facing each other now, lying on our sides as the sun beats down on us. “That's a great way of looking at it.”

“So, what are your flaws?”

Max trails his hand in the sand, letting it run through his fingers. “I'm not sure that telling you all this is a good idea before you know all my great points.”

“You can start with those.”

“Well, I'm better in bed than either of my brothers,” he laughs.

“That would be quite an achievement,” I say.

“Well, I have some help.” His tone is cryptic, and he winks, daring me to ask.

I trail my hand in the hot sand too, realizing too late that I'm mimicking his body language, something that should tell him that I'm attracted to him if he didn't already know. “What help?”

“You ever seen a Prince Albert?”

My eyes widen because I know what he's talking about. Max laughs again, maybe he's used to the kind of reaction his piercing elicits. “I haven't.”

“So, I guess that means you've never experienced one?”

“No again.”

"Interesting," he says. "Or it would be, for both of us."

"You Banbury men are very presumptuous."

His hand reaches out for mine, and he links fingers with me. "Maybe not presumptuous but hopeful, and you have had fun with two men who are pretty identical to me, so I don't think it's that farfetched to imagine that you might think I'm sexy enough to take to bed."

"Looks are only ever a small part," I say.

"So, what attracted you to Mason?"

"The way he treated me. His artistic nature. His lack of arrogance about his talent. His acceptance when I turned him down."

"You turned him down? I didn't hear that part."

"I did…not because of anything he did. More because of where I am right now."

"And where's that?"

"I don't really know. That was part of the reason."

Max nods, still holding onto my hand. "And Miller?"

"Well, you know that was initially an accident?"

At that moment, there are shouts from the shoreline where one of the brothers is celebrating beating the other. Max rolls his eyes. "They're still as competitive as they were when we were kids."

"Just not about sex?"

"Mason laughed his ass off when he heard that Miller got laid as a case of mistaken identity. Although we're pretty chill about sex, there still is some healthy competition between us."

"Is that why you're holding my hand? You're feeling competitive that you're the only one who hasn't…"

"Tasted you. Yeah. I'm feeling like that isn't really a situation that should exist for any longer than it has to."

"But I can't just switch it on," I say. "I mean, you're a sexy guy…and the tattoos…well, the package is great, but I don't know you enough to have those feelings yet. I'm sorry."

Max squeezes my fingers gently, and then let's go as though he senses he needs to give me some space. "There's no rush, Natalie. I was joking about that. This isn't a competition between us, and as much as I'd love to know why my brothers seem to have lost their sense over you, I only want that when it's something you're ready for." I nod, and he rubs his shoulder, just above a tattoo of an eagle that crowns his bicep and shoulder. "I get why Mason played the game with you."

"He told you about that. Is that something he does a lot?" Only part of me wants to know the answer to that question because the other part is aching with jealousy.

"Not a lot…we had a girlfriend in college…she was a friend of the family. We came up with the game because we wanted to be sure that she was leading everything. We were young and scared that it could end badly…you know with false accusations."

"Wow…I never thought of that. Was that why Mason played the game with me?"

"No…that was about you facing up to and expressing what you want."

"Yeah, that was what I thought."

"Is that not something you're good at?"

I shrug. "Not really."

I'm about to ask more about Max when my phone begins to ring. "Sorry," I say, searching around in my purse. When I see the caller ID, I hesitate, lowering the phone as my heart begins to race.

Nate.

What the hell does he want? I certainly didn't leave him with any expectation that we would remain on speaking terms. When I left, I didn't even say goodbye. Surely he got the message that I was leaving him for good with no intention of looking back.

"Who is it?" Max asks. I guess my hesitation must look strange.

"My ex."

"Are you on bad terms?"

"You could say that."

"Could it be an emergency of some sort?"

I can't think of anything, but I guess there might be something. Maybe something happened to a mutual friend of ours, or maybe something happened to Nate. I swipe to accept the call, needing to be sure that nothing serious is happening.

"Hello."

There's a pause on the other end of the line. "Natalie. I wasn't sure you'd pick up."

"What is it, Nate?"

"I just wanted to check you were okay…you left very abruptly when you were in a very emotionally unbalanced state. I was very distressed for you, but I didn't know what to do. I hope you've managed to calm down."

"Is that all?"

Nate makes a funny sound in his throat that sounds as though he's stifling a laugh. Of course, he'd find my coolness amusing. It's his way of undermining me in a way so subtle that it's almost imperceptible, except I see it now. I see all of his awful manipulative ways.

"You know this attitude doesn't suit you at all, Natalie. You're more feminine than this…have you changed your contraceptive pill? You know that can make you unstable."

"Unstable?" I can't help the anger that bubbles up and into my voice at Nate's accusation, or the way it makes me sit up straight and ball my fist.

"Cambodia is lovely, Natalie. You know I could get you a flight out tomorrow, and we could complete the itinerary you worked so hard on. This was your dream…the Natalie I know and love wouldn't throw all this away over a rumor."

"Rumor? You told me what happened. You told me that you slept with those women because I wouldn't do what you wanted in the bedroom." As I spit that sentence, I see Max flinch. His eyes have darkened while he listens, his fists now clenched at his sides.

"It was for you, Natalie. I know that you're struggling to see that, but that's because you have such a narrow way of looking at the world. If you just broadened your horizons…"

"My horizons are broad enough, Nate. I'm not coming out to Cambodia, and I don't want to listen to any more of this, okay?"

"No, it's not okay. You listen to me. You made a commitment to me, and this…your tantrum is costing me money. I'm booking you a flight, and you need to get out here, or there'll be consequences."

I pull the phone away from my ear, eyes fixed on it in disbelief. There's the switch I've become so accustomed to with Nate; nice one minute and cutting the next. What is he going to do? He's still ranting on the phone, but I can't hear what he's saying…just the tone is enough to make my heart race in the horrible panicky way that Nate has always managed to cause. I pull in a shuddery breath.

"Are you okay?" Max says.

Those three words of kindness are enough to spill the tears I've been trying so hard to hold back.

That's the trigger for Max. He grabs the phone out of my hand. "Listen!" he shouts. "I don't know who the fuck you are, and I don't really care. You need to calm the fuck down and hang up this call right now before I find out who you are and where you are, and I come and show you what happens to assholes who speak to women that way."

Max doesn't give Nate time to respond. He just pokes his finger at the screen to end the call and places it on the lounger next to me.

"When did you break up?" Max asks. There's a clipped sound to his speech, and when I raise my eyes from my knees to look at him, his jaw ticks with tension.

"A few days ago." The time since I returned has passed so fast that it's hard to reconcile that this is actually true. When my feet hit U.S. soil, Nate was a big looming pain-causing specter in my life. Since meeting the Banbury triplets, he's shrunken down to a small sharp stone in my shoe. But that call has brought everything back in the worst way.

"I'm sorry I had to do that, Natalie. I wouldn't normally wade into someone else's private life that way, but the way that dude was talking to you was not okay, and I'm not prepared to sit by while you get upset like that."

"It's okay," I say, although it really isn't. I'm not angry with Max at all. In fact, his actions really show me what kind of man he is, and that's a good one. I just know that for Nate, being told off like that will be a big deal. A big enough deal that he'll be furious beyond proportion. A shiver of nervousness runs through me at the very thought that this could all escalate.

"Hey. It's okay." Max places his big warm hand on my knee. "He's not going to bother you again. Trust me."

I wipe my eyes with the back of my hand. "You don't know, Nate. He doesn't like to be told what to do, and he doesn't like it when he feels that someone is getting one over on him."

"He's controlling?"

I nod and watch Max's expression harden. "And violent?"

"No. He was never violent."

"With his hands, you mean. He was plenty violent with his words and actions."

That's a way of thinking about how Nate treated me that hasn't occurred to me before, but I'm mortified that Max knows all of this about me. It was a stupid thing to do. I shouldn't have taken that call in front of him. What must he think of me now? A frigid angry girl who can't keep her boyfriend satisfied. A weak girl who can't stand up for herself and needs a practical stranger to swoop in to fix her problems. He'll tell his brothers, and they'll all pity me for being pathetic.

Max squeezes my knee. "I think we should go for a swim now. Wash off that douchebag. He doesn't deserve your tears or your worry, okay? It's over."

"I hope so."

Max stands and reaches for my hand. When he takes hold of it to help me up, he does it with all the care and grace of a true gentleman. He may be covered in tattoos and piercings, and he might have a job that makes him a tough guy, but underneath all that, Max is the kind of man who knows how to treat a woman.

"Come on."

We walk toward the shore, and Max drops my hand, throwing his arm around my shoulder and tugging me against his body. It's the kind of hug that tells me that I'm under his protection now. Brotherly, in a way, not that I'd really know what having a brother was like. When I was little, I used to imagine how it would feel to have siblings; a sister I could play house with and a brother who'd beat up the bullies at school.

Now I have three stepbrothers who are so huge and strong that they could defend me against pretty much anything. Mason and Miller stop their game and watch our approach. They share intrigued smiles, maybe wondering if Max has used his time alone with me wisely.

"We're gonna swim," Max says.

"About time. I'm overheating," Miller says. He drops his paddle on the sand and jogs into the sea, creating waves of spray on either side of him. When he's deep enough, he disappears, surfacing with water trailing over his skin and messy hair that he sweeps backward. Mason shakes his head, walking into the sea more calmly, at the same pace as Max and me.

"He always loves to make an entrance."

"More like a spectacle," Max laughs.

"Well, I thought it was very impressive," I say.

"See?" Miller puffs out his chest, and he laughs.

"Don't start with that," Max says, shaking his head. "Miller has a big enough head without you flattering him with your attention."

The sea is cold around my thighs, and I stop, scooping some to trail over my skin to make getting under the water easier. When I look up, three pairs of eyes are all fixed on my wet skin. "You guys are looking at me like you've never seen a woman before."

"There's only one woman I want to be looking at right now," Mason says.

"There's only one woman worth looking at," Miller says.

"You guys have had more than your fair share of looking," Max says with a scowl that is so disgruntled, I splutter with laughter.

"Maybe Natalie would be happy to remedy that," Mason says with a wink.

"In what way?"

"Well, we're all alone out here." We all look around to confirm that there isn't another person in view. "And maybe you could show him just a little of what he's missed out on."

"How?"

Mason comes up behind me, putting his hands on my shoulders and running them down my arms. Even in the cold ocean, his hands are still warm, and I shiver. What I didn't notice is that he's slid the straps of my bikini top down with his thumbs, and as he gently tugs, the swell of my breasts becomes more obvious. "Hey," I say, putting my hands up to keep everything in place.

He bends to kiss my neck and whispers, "Just a little look…nothing else."

My eyes meet Max's, which have gone from clear-sky blue to the darkest navy with just the thought of seeing what's beneath my hands. My nipples have hardened into points pinched by arousal.

Miller moves closer, the dynamic between us all as static as electricity.

"We can't," I say.

Max nods, letting me know he understands, and Mason's hands lower. "Okay," he says softly.

There's no anger in Max's voice or frustration in his expression. I said no, and they listened and accepted. Just like in Mason's studio, their willingness to let me decide without pressure is the biggest turn-on. How easy is it for them to make me feel as though my voice counts, my feelings are important? How easy is it for them to show me why everything about my relationship with Nate was toxic and wrong?

I turn my head, and Mason smiles that brilliant smile of his, dimples and all. "You can't blame me for trying," he says.

Miller splashes his brother, and Max laughs, and somewhere in all that joy, I have the same feeling of freedom that led to me having sex with Mason and Miller. With no force or expectation, they make me see that I get to decide.

I fix my gaze on Max, slowly removing my hands from my chest. The straps of my bikini tickle my elbows, but instead of using them to draw my top down, I reach behind to unclip the fastening. The sounds of laughter and splashing die down to a stillness that comes with the greatest anticipation, and when I peel away the wet fabric from my skin, baring my breasts to Max, I feel like a completely different person.

# 18

Where does freedom come from?

It exists not only outside of us but inside too. We create our own chains to deal with our insecurities. We hold ourselves back for fear of what others will think of us or what we will think of ourselves.

I thought I was free when I first booked my flights to see the world: just me and my camera, and Nate, of course. I'd never stepped outside of the big ol' USA. I'd never actually been out of my own state. Holding a passport felt like freedom. Eating new food and spending time in new cultures felt like freedom too, but looking back on it all, it was just on the surface. Inside I was holding myself in a tightly wrapped bow, holding myself back so that Nate would approve of me, keeping guard on my own impulses so as never to push myself too much further than he would accept.

As I stand between these three men, all of that seems to slide away.

What is freedom? It's existing in a place where your mind and body are your own. It's the sense of peace that comes with accepting what Miller spoke about. Each step is just progression on a long journey. Whether it's positive or negative, it still moves us forward. That propulsion is inevitable. We can't fight it by restricting ourselves. By doing that we just take different steps that don't feel as good.

I want to take my life's steps with conviction. I want to take steps that will broaden my horizons, not narrow them like I did when I was with Nate.

Every step I take that involves Mason, Miller, and Max seems to fill me inside. I feel bigger and brighter when I'm with them. I feel confident and exuberant.

I feel free.

Max says nothing for the longest time. His eyes don't leave my breasts, but I can see what he's thinking by the way he bites on his bottom lip. There's a hungriness about him that warms me between the legs. He rubs his shoulder again, the eagle appearing and disappearing behind his hand.

"Natalie." His voice is husky. "Come here."

"That's not how the game works," Mason says softly, still standing behind me. "Natalie knows she makes all the decisions."

"Come here," I say to Max, turning the tables.

He moves through the water with the grace of a panther, and I inhale a little sharp burst of breath when his hand grasps my hip beneath the water.

"You have no idea how sexy you look," Max says. "Look…"

He takes my hand and presses it over the rigid bar of his cock, nudging my thumb over the metallic bead that must be his piercing. Oh God, he feels big, just like his brothers. We both look down as he lets go of my hand. I don't want to let go of him. Not right away, at least. I want to stroke him until I see his eyes roll, and I feel his cock thicken even more.

Mason and Miller step closer, drawn to what we're doing out in the open. I've never been this brazen. I've never had the desire or courage to be sexual in public.

"That feels good," Max says.

"It'd feel even better skin to skin," Miller says.

"That's up to Natalie."

I look between these men who are like three demigods, hewn from rock. So tall and broad, with biceps made to hold me and chests perfect to cradle me against. Eyes like jewels and smiles that light up everything around them. I look, and I can't work out how I have gotten so lucky. At a push, I might just be enough for one of them if I really work hard to be the best me that I can be, but for three of them? I don't see it, but I want to try.

I really want to try.

"Take me back to the house," I say. "And show me what you boys can do."

# 19

The walk back to the beach house is filled with laughter and peppered by silences laced with anticipation. I see the looks that pass between my stepbrothers, but there is nothing there that makes me think that I should change my mind about what I'm about to do.

Mom and Conrad are away on business. The house is empty except for the staff, and none of them has to know anything. In the safety of my room, I'm free to experience. I'm free to give myself over to three men who feel like my awakening.

I lead them up the stairs, feeling their eyes on my body as I take step after step closer to living a fantasy.

Connie would never believe I'd be capable of this. Up until just now, neither did I!

The air-conditioning is doing its work to keep everything perfectly ambient, but I miss the natural feel of outside, so I throw open my balcony door allowing the breeze and sound of the waves to drift in. When I turn, Max is closing the door behind him, then turning the lock, the click is punctuation separating who I was before and who I will become. My skin is sticky from the sea and the sun-cream, but I don't care. Gone are the days when I felt it was necessary to wash and shave myself to perfection for a man.

These men don't make me feel like my body is anything to be ashamed of — quite the opposite.

I don't wait for them to make the first move because that's not who I am anymore. I'm a new Natalie. Confident Natalie. The kind of woman who removes her swimwear in a room filled with three gorgeous men and stands naked before them expectantly.

Mason and Miller both told me that they're not jealous of their brothers, and I see that when they wait for Max to step forward first. They could be eager and selfish, but they aren't. Instead, they're watchful and considerate.

"Are you sure this is what you want," Max asks.

"I'm naked," I say with a smile. "I think I've just confirmed what I want by stripping off my clothes."

"I still want to hear it. I still want you to tell me what you need."

"Show me your cock," I say, with no hesitation or shame. "Show me what I touched but didn't get to see."

He hooks his thumbs into the waistband of his swim shorts and tugs them down in one smooth gesture. His cock springs free, tapping his belly, the piercing glinting in the sunlight streaming through the window. My eyes widen as I take in the intricate tattoo that covers his cock.

"I didn't know you could ink there too," I say. "That must have been so painful."

Max takes hold of his cock, rubbing his thumb across the Prince Albert, tugging it harder than I ever would have felt comfortable doing. "Pain isn't something to be afraid of. It's all just mind over matter. You want to touch it, skin to skin?"

"Yeah," I say, stepping until I'm close enough to wrap my hand around the most mind-blowing cock I've ever seen. It's not just about size. Mason and Miller have identically huge cocks, and I've spent time with them in my hand, mouth and pussy. It's about the way Max has decorated this private part of his body. I never thought it would be something I'd be into, but damn, the intricate black spirals that circle his cock are such a turn on. There's something primal about it, maybe because I know to suffer through its pain makes him tougher than I could ever be.

The feel of his skin there is hotter than I expect. Everything about Max is hot, from his undulating abs to his muscular thighs. Even his feet are sexy, and that is not something I've thought about before…ever!

I glance around, finding Miller and Mason watching the movement of my hand and for the first time in my life, I don't feel self-conscious. There's no judgment here. No expectation that I have to live up to. These men are so chill with each other and with me. They live life as though they're just happy to be around to participate.

And participate, they will.

Did I know that I'd be turned on by them watching me? Not until this moment.

I get an urge to drop to my knees to serve Max in a way I never have with any man before. There's no power struggle here, and that's what makes me feel comfortable enough to submit. The rug is soft on my knees, and Max groans in pleasure as I use my tongue to circle the head of his cock, relishing his piercing's coolness in my mouth. He hisses, his hand sliding into my hair but not gripping. It's not about him controlling my actions at all. Instead, he caresses me gently, sending the nerves buzzing across my scalp.

"That looks so fucking hot," Miller says. He's moved closer and is now sitting on the bed's edge, his cock in his hand.

I gaze into Max's eyes and feel his cock kick in my mouth, the eye contact turning him on even more. Mason kneels beside me, kissing my shoulders, and my neck, running his fingers down my back and over the bare flesh of my ass. I want him to touch me while I do this, something that would be impossible if there was only one man in this room with me. I guess this is the benefit of more than one set of hands, of more than one cock. There doesn't need to be any downtime, no matter what I'm doing. Then it hits me. Three men to please is actually three men to please me. I draw back from Max, using the slickness from my mouth to lubricate the movements of my hand.

"Touch me," I tell Mason, and he does, stroking over my belly and between my legs, finding me wetter than I was expecting.

"You like that, don't you? You like kneeling for my brother and sucking his cock."

I nod, licking out again until Max's hand starts to tremble.

"Do you like being watched?" Miller asks. He's dropped to his knees too, his fingers finding my nipples and pinching them with just the right amount of pressure.

"Yes," I say, but that one affirmative doesn't really cover how I feel right now. Between these three huge men, I feel tiny but at the same time powerful. It's strange that something that most people would imagine would be degrading is actually uplifting. Mason works another finger inside me, then another until I'm stuffed with his twisting hand, moaning onto Max's cock while Miller strokes me like I'm precious and beautiful.

"Tell us what you want," Max says, cupping my chin in his big warm hand.

"I want you to show me what you'd do if you had complete control."

"You want us to be in charge?" Max's eyebrows raise. I guess he wasn't expecting that.

"Complete control within reason," I smile. "If I don't like anything, I'll tell you."

"You have to promise," Miller says. "If there's even a chance that you won't, then we won't go any further. There has to be total trust for this to work."

"I will," I say. "You and Mason, you've shown me how to have a voice. You prepared me."

"Okay, baby," Max says, bending down to pick me up as though I weigh nothing. I'm dumped onto the bed with a laughing Max crawling over me, holding both my hands above my head. "You want us to be in control."

Staring up at his handsome face, I nod. "I've never done anything like this before. I wouldn't know what to ask for. I wouldn't know how to choreograph something so intimate with so many people."

"It's not a dance," Miller says. "But, I get what you mean."

"Anyway, there's something very sexy about being manhandled by three strong, sexy men."

"So you want to be manhandled," Mason says. "Gently or roughly?"

"Surprise me." In my filthy little heart, I'm hoping for the rough, and that takes me by surprise. I've never wanted a man's hands or actions to be harsh before, so it must be something about these men that gives me confidence. I know they could make me feel things I've never felt before and come out the other side whole and not broken.

Max wastes no time in opening my legs wide and notching his cock at my entrance. I gaze down between our bodies, marveling at the way his darkly patterned cock looks against the pink of my pussy. His piercing is already inside me, and I brace myself for the unfamiliar sensation it might cause as he drives deep inside me.

Oh god. My eyes roll as he spreads me wide, the wetness Mason's fingers generated slicking his way. He pumps deep a few times, taking my ankles in his big hands, holding them as wide as they'll go. He's such a big, muscular man that my narrow hips struggle to take him.

"That's it," Miller says. "Fuck her deep. Make her feel it."

My clit tingles, his words like a feather over my most sensitive place.

"Miller, you take her mouth," Mason orders, and his brother wastes no time. I expect him to come to my side, but he straddles my head from behind, tipping my chin back, so my head is a little off the edge of the bed. When he slides his cock into my open mouth, Max thrust harder, jerking me towards Mason, so his cock pushes deeper and deeper into my throat. My eyes start to water, but I'm buzzing. So lightheaded that I can almost see the image of myself from above; a girl who's let so many inhibitions go to seek the ultimate release. Miller's thumb strokes my cheeks and pulls out, the sight of my tears too much.

"Turn her over," he says, throwing himself onto his back and then tugging me into his lap. "That's it, baby. You okay?"

I nod, bending to kiss his full lips as Max climbs onto the bed behind me. "We're going to try something," he says, the huskiness of his voice giving away exactly how turned on he is. "If it's too much, you just let us know."

Miller tugs at my hips, sliding me onto his big, waiting cock, then he pulls me down onto his chest. I start to undulate my hips, the feeling of him inside me driving me on, but he grips my ass tightly. "Still, Natalie. Max is gonna come in too."

"Where?" I gasp, gazing into Miller's hooded eyes.

"Your pussy," he says matter of factly like it's the most obvious thing in the world.

My gasp sets Miller laughing. "You think we're too big?"

"I think I'm too small," I say.

"You will stretch," Max says, spitting into his palm and lubricating his cock.

The first push seems impossible. I flinch, and Mason kisses my mouth, telling me to relax in between kisses. Max's hand strokes my back, down my spine and lower, grazing my taint. I flinch again, the sensations so overwhelming and forbidden that I don't know how else to react.

"It's okay," Max says, pushing again. This time, the pierced head of his cock managed to penetrate me just an inch. Oh…it feels good. Crazy good. I'm stretched beyond what I ever could have imagined, and my clit pressed tightly against Mason buzzes with stimulation.

"Relax," Max says, his hand on my ass stroking gently as though he's quieting a skittish horse.

I close my eyes and breathe in Miller's scent, imagining the waves lapping on the shore outside our window. Max pushes deeper, and I exhale with it until he's as deep as he can get.

"Fuck," Miller says. He grips my hair and twists my face towards his. I open my eyes, and he smiles down at me. "See. You can take it. You can take it all."

And I can. Oh, I can.

"Can you take me too?" Mason asks. "Here." He strokes my bottom lip with this thumb, pulling it down to open my mouth.

I nod, and he replaces his thumb with this cock, and then his brothers start to move.

I lose myself in their movements' rhythm, the push and pull so mesmerizing that time seems to slip. I would never have believed that I could come this way, with so much happening to my body all at once. But an orgasm starts to build, welling from deep in my belly and spreading across my clit, making me buck against Miller. I groan against Mason, and the vibrations are enough to make him spill into my mouth, accompanied by groans of his own. Miller and Max aren't far behind; their combined orgasms squashing me between their sweat-slicked muscular bodies.

And amongst all of this overwhelmingly filthy activity, a laugh bubbles inside me that I can't subdue. It rocks my body so hard that I'm shaking against Miller. For a second, I wonder how my stepbrothers will react. Will they think I'm crazy? Then they start to laugh too, kissing my shoulders and my cheeks, and Max pats my ass as he withdraws.

"That was…" I say, but there are too many words that could end that sentence for me to choose just one. Amazing. Exhilarating. Mind-blowing. Overwhelming. Passionate. But what I want to say is 'an awakening'. I feel as though I've slept through everything that came before in my life, and now I'm finally conscious.

"It was," Miller says, and I think they must feel it too.

# 20

It's early evening when Max has to leave for the start of his shift. He showers in my bathroom while I rest between his brothers, then climbs onto the bed, smelling deliciously fresh, to kiss me goodbye.

"Look after her," he instructs his brothers, and they nod solemnly like they've been entrusted with a vitally important task. "I'll see you later," he says, pausing to look at me as he leaves the room, then closing the door behind him.

I must fall asleep because it's morning when I wake, and Max is sitting in a chair dressed in his black suit, sipping a cup of strong coffee.

"Are you back already?" I whisper. The room is glowing with the rising sun, and Miller and Mason are still sleeping.

He nods. "It was quiet. I asked one of my team to cover for me. I didn't want to stay away for too long."

"That's good. Come back to bed."

Max shakes his head. "There isn't enough room, and you guys will be getting up soon. I need to get some sleep."

I wriggle out from beneath Mason's arm and shuffle off the end of the bed as carefully as I can. "I'll come with you," I say.

Max pulls me onto his lap, resting his coffee cup on the floor. I lean in to kiss his warm mouth, and he holds me close. "You know if you come, I'm not going to get any sleep at all."

"I'll be good. I promise."

"Okay then. You'd better put something on, though." He pats my bare ass, looking down at my body appreciatively. "And if you're good, I'll give you something really good for breakfast."

"You mean lunch," I say, standing to search for my pretty white cotton shorts and camisole pajamas.

"It's all a matter of perspective," he says.

I follow Max through the house, ascending another flight of stairs and passing through another corridor. He opens the door to his room, which is the same size as mine but decorated for a bachelor. There's a low black leather sofa in the place of my chair and a dark wood sleigh bed whereas mine is colonial painted wood. It smells of his cologne and is very tidy, a reflection of his focus and discipline.

"I'm gonna freshen up," he says. "Jump on in."

The sheets on his bed are crisp and fresh, the mattress perfectly firm. He's quick in the bathroom and returns in his underwear, hanging his work clothes before joining me.

"I'm beat," he says softly, kissing my forehead. "But you are the best thing I've come home to in a long time."

I stroke my fingers over his shoulder, observing his ink up close. "This eagle is amazing," I say. "It's like a photo."

"My friend did all my ink. He's very talented."

"Why an eagle?"

"It's a symbol of strength," Max says. "But also of freedom. For a long time, I felt like I had to be a certain person to fulfill the expectations of my family. Mom had always encouraged us all to join Dad's business. She wanted us to be professionals. To study law, accounting, and business and slide seamlessly into our father's shoes. When she died, we were thirteen. It was the time when we were starting to find the things that interested us, but also the time when we didn't feel like we could do anything to disrupt the status quo. Dad was broken, and just about holding it together. He needed us to hold onto the dreams he shared with Mom as a way of fulfilling her legacy."

"I understand that," I say. "It must have been so hard."

"It was…mostly because I knew that being myself would have hurt my dad. I didn't want to sit in a stuffy office poring over numbers or legal jargon. I didn't want to live in my dad's shadow, and I'd spent enough time with my brothers to know that we needed to find separate paths if we were ever going to keep our close bond. Love needs space to breathe."

I nod, thinking about how wise Max sounds. Wise like the eagle.

"When did you tell your dad?"

"When I was eighteen. I'd been taking martial arts classes in the evening. I was already pretty strong. I knew I wanted to go into the police or secret service…something that would be different every day, where I wouldn't be fixed in one place but meeting people and keeping them safe. Standing up to my dad was a rite of passage. I marked myself with the eagle to remember that freedom comes at a price. I had to disappoint him to make him proud, and he is now. With time he can see that it was right for me."

"And your brothers?"

"They did the same. Three sons and none of them wanted to run the family business. I guess when Dad can't do it anymore, we'll take the reins as directors but leave the day-to-day to others. Or maybe we'll sell it. Who knows? At least Dad understands that we aren't rejecting him by rejecting the dream he built."

"And this one?" I trail my finger down his center until I brush the bulge of his cock beneath his underwear.

"The patterns are Maori. It's the Koru. The symbol of new beginnings, or new life."

"That's very literal," I say.

"I can be a very literal guy."

He smooths his hand over my hair in a way that feels protective. "Do you think your ex will call you again?"

"I don't know," I say. "I didn't think he'd call me at all. Now I have no idea what he'll do."

"I want you to tell me about every interaction you have with him from now on, okay? Phone calls, messages, social media, email…in person."

"He's in Cambodia." There's safety in knowing that he's far away.

"Maybe he is," Max says. "You don't really know that for sure."

"I guess."

"I just…I have a sense of this kind of thing. I guess it comes with the territory. Just promise you'll tell me everything, okay? Even things that don't seem serious."

"Okay." I know he's just trying to keep me safe, but his concern has unsettled me.

"Hey," he says, taking my hand beneath the covers. "You don't need to worry about anything. We've got your back, baby. It's in our hands now."

It has been a long time since I felt that anyone had my back. In fact, I'm wondering if there has ever been a time when I've felt truly safe and supported. My mom did her best, but I always felt that we were exposed without a father in the picture. Even in relationships, there has always been an element of uncertainty for me, but there are no feelings like that in Max's arms. Here, all I feel is security.

I kiss his lips gently, observing the darkness circling his eyes and feeling so grateful that I've found him, even if it is for a short time. "You need to get some sleep now."

"I do," he says with a sleepy smile. "Goodnight, princess. See you in the morning."

I blink as Max falls asleep in front of me, as though someone flicked his off switch. I lie awake, listening to his rhythmic breathing, keeping a watch on a strong and brave man who has marked his body with his steps to freedom and a new start.

And now this man and his brothers have enabled me to see what I've been missing.

I don't know how I'm going to find a way to remember these days when I finally spread my wings, but I'll find a way.

# 21

I wake earlier than Max, but I don't want to disturb him, so I lie quietly, listening to him breathe for a while before I pluck up the courage to try to slip out of bed. I pad downstairs to my room, which I find empty. Either Mason and Miller left the bed perfectly made, or the housekeeper has completed her rounds early. I shower quickly, finding my white two-piece and pretty blue paisley sarong. With nothing else to do today, the beach is calling my name.

Downstairs, the boys are nowhere to be seen, and I'm sorry about that because I was looking forward to seeing them. Maybe they had other things to do today. None of us are at the point of sharing our timetables.

How is it that we've gotten to the point of sharing bodily fluids but not our mundane plans? It should feel back to front, but it doesn't. It just feels good. Flashes of last night come back to me, complete with the inevitable blush, putting my hand to my mouth to trap the relived sensation of kisses against my lips. On the deck, the table is set with breakfast items and a pot of coffee and tea.

How easy would it be to get used to his kind of life? Easier than I imagined.

I take a seat, helping myself to a big blueberry muffin and some fresh berries. The coffee pours with steam that tells me its fresh. Two used plates confirm that Miller and Mason have already eaten, and then I hear the distant shout of voices from the beach. They didn't leave to run errands. They're spending the day here too.

I'm rushing through my food when hands cover my eyes, and lips press the top of my head. "Guess who?" a deep voice says.

"Max!"

"You can tell us apart already," he says, dropping to the seat next to me.

"Nah…I just know your brothers are already down on the beach."

Max grabs a croissant and pours his coffee black. "Even our dad used to struggle to identify us. It's easier now I have these." He brushes his hand over his inked arm.

"Is that one of the reasons you got the tattoos?"

He tears the pastry and pops some into his mouth, chewing thoughtfully. "Not consciously. It never bothered me that I was one of three. It's always seemed like a positive thing. I love my brothers, so being mistaken for them wasn't something I'd feel angry about. It was fun, messing with our parents and our tutors."

"And your friends?"

"Friends were something that happened later when we insisted on going to school. Even then, I think people found it tough to break into our circle because we were so tight."

"I haven't found it hard," I smile.

"That is true." Max rests his hand on my knee and squeezes. "I don't know why but sometimes people come into our lives who just fit. There's no explaining it. There's no understanding it. It's just luck."

"Or fate," I say.

Max shrugs. He's more down to earth than that. Believing in fate is like believing in God or aliens. You can't see it. It's something you feel. The pull or push of unseen forces. Coincidences that are just too difficult to put down to something that isn't spiritual.

Why did I meet these men? It was a chain of events with no start that I can pinpoint. What puts us in the right place at the right time? Decisions made before we were born affect where we wind up. If Mom hadn't met Conrad, and if Nate hadn't fucked around, and if Connie hadn't put me forward to take photographs none of this would have happened. If Mason hadn't accepted the modeling job or Miller had traveled to work in New York instead of setting up a practice here or if Max had decided to join the military instead of working in security, things would have been so different for us all.

"Whatever it is, I'm happy it's happened."

"Me too."

We finish our breakfast quickly, the lure of the beach too much for either of us. Max tells me stories from his shift last night; the card counter, the pickpocket, and the chip snatcher. They even had a VIP to protect, but he won't tell me who. It's reassuring to me that he's discreet about his work.

He slings his arm around my shoulders as we stroll down to the beach, and kisses my forehead when I tell him a funny story about when I was a little girl. Mason and

Miller greet us warmly when we finally have sand between our toes.

"You stole our girl," Miller says, punching his brother's shoulder. "I woke up with this asshole's face next to mine on the pillow." He waves his arm at Mason in disgust.

"She came willingly," Max says, hugging me against him. "I think it's the tattoos. She likes a bad boy."

"Is that right? Better tell me who your tattoo artist is then," Mason says.

"You'd ink yourself for me?" I'm horrified, even though I'm pretty sure he's joking.

"Nah," Mason laughs. "I like this plain old skin too much."

"And no one could create something as beautiful as one of your paintings," I say.

Miller nods. "Exactly. When you have art in your blood, accepting someone else's design must be that much harder."

"So what are we doing today?" Miller asks.

"We're sunbathing, and swimming, playing cards, and reading," I say.

"Better add in some eating and drinking," Mason says.

"And fucking," Miller adds.

"Definitely fucking," Max says, pinching my ass. He gets a slap on his ridiculous thick bicep for that, although the fucking will undoubtedly be my favorite part of the day. In fact, I'm not even really sure why we're down here on the beach when there are more than ten bedrooms upstairs that we could be messing up. The thought sends a rush of heat between my legs and over my cheeks.

"Natalie is thinking about the fucking," Miller says. He takes my hand and tugs me forward, grabbing hold of my ass and planting a kiss firmly on my lips. "It's okay. I'm thinking about it too."

"And me." Mason puts his hand over his cock and gives it a squeeze.

"And me." Max comes behind me and bends to kiss my neck softly. As Miller releases my ass from his grip, Max presses against me so I can feel the solidness of his very thick, very long, very erect cock against my flesh.

My breathing speeds, the heat of being sandwiched this way, and knowing how easy it would be to move into more has me flustered. This beach is private, these men are willing, and I am wet. So wet it's almost embarrassing.

"Can we do some of the other things before the fucking?" I say, trying to make my tone as lighthearted as possible.

"Of course," Miller plants a kiss on my lips that is laced with a sweet smile.

"Race you to the ocean," Miller says, kicking off his sliders.

"Always a fucking competition," Mason says, but he's already running.

If breasts weren't a thing, I'd be running after them, pushing my hardest to hit that water first, but this swimsuit is not up to dealing with that much bouncing.

"Shall we walk?" Max rolls his eyes at his brothers and slides his hand into mine.

We mess around in the shallows, spending time talking about anything and everything. It reminds me of my last year at high school when I finally starting to get comfortable socializing. A big group of us would hang out wherever we could – the skate park, the mall, or the football field – to share stories about when we were kids, and our ideas and plans for the future. Those days were about remembering where we came from but recognizing that we would soon be moving forward. With Mason, Max, and Miller, it feels similar.

As I share stories of my past and learn more about theirs, tiny strands of connection are formed that by themselves wouldn't mean a thing but layered begin to form a bond. We share the grief of losing a parent too young, and I see the fractured part of them as they talk about their mom. It makes me want to pull them all into my arms to give them the love and affection they missed out on.

“I'm so sorry about your mom,” I say. “I'm sure your dad was great, and he obviously did a great job at raising you right, but it's tough to be without a mom's warmth.”

“It was,” Mason says. “It still is. Do you ever catch yourself wondering what they'd think of you if they were still alive? Like, would she be happy with how I turned out?”

“I'm pretty certain she would be,” I say. “I think the same about my dad. He'd be disappointed at what happened with my ex. I know that for sure.”

“No father wants to see their daughter with a douchebag,” Max says. “But the disappointment wouldn't be on you, Natalie. The anger and frustration would rest with Nate.”

“You really think that?”

“Yeah, of course. You need to stop blaming yourself for trusting another human being who lied to you and deceived you.”

“I guess.”

"No guessing about it." Max takes hold of my hand under the water and brings it to his lips. "Your dad would think you're too precious for someone to manipulate you that way."

"What do you think your mom would think of me? A girl who's taken all of her sons to bed at once."

Miller shakes his head and shrugs. "I'm pretty certain she'd have loved you. You're actually similar in some ways…and I hope that doesn't sound weird."

"How are we similar?"

"She was little like you, and for a while, when we were young, she had short hair too, but I think it's something about the way you move your hands and the way you smile."

"I can see that," Mason says.

"But I bet she wouldn't think much of me after last night."

"Our parents are from another generation," Max says. "But don't forget that despite their more traditional values, the 1960s was all free love and experimental sex. They just got married and forgot all about it."

"Is that what this is? Experimental sex?"

"What would you like it to be?" Miller asks. Of course, he would turn the tables and put it on me to define what's happening here – typical shrink to answer a question with another question.

I don't answer straight away because I can sense the importance of this moment in determining what happens next between us. I have no idea how these men really feel about me, outside of liking to spend time together and enjoying the fucking. Those are good and necessary parts of any relationship between a man and a woman, but do they want more? Is "more" even a thing?

"I'd like it to be a thing that makes me happy," I say. "I need happy in my life."

"And do we make you happy?" Mason asks.

"Yes. Very. But what would you like this to be?"

The triplets look between each other, and I sense that they're weighing the moment in much the same way as I did. Maybe they're thinking that acting too cool could push me away, but too eager for more could as well. The beginnings of relationships involve so much tiptoeing around that it can be very frustrating.

Max clears his throat. "We're looking for someone to…" He glances at Miller, who nods. Either they're really good at the sibling mind-reading thing, or they've actually talked about this. "…for someone to…"

"Be with us like this for good," Mason finishes.

Max seems to exhale with relief that the pressure is off him just as I breathe in so fast that I feel lightheaded. "You want an arrangement like this for the long term?"

Miller nods. "We've tried it in other ways. We've dated separately, and it just doesn't feel right being so divided from my brothers."

"Relationships take up a lot of time, and that is generally time spent apart. It just doesn't make us happy." Mason runs his fingers through his hair, pushing it back from where it was flopping in his eyes. There's something about the gesture that is self-conscious.

"Women either want to keep us apart, or they have a fetish thing about flirting with the ones they're not in a relationship with, which becomes awkward."

"Yeah, I get that."

"So this is where it feels right. One woman who knows the score, who wants us all as much as we want her."

I don't know what to feel. I know how lucky I am to have met these amazing men. I know how many women would jump into my shoes at this moment and embrace this crazy situation for a lifetime. I know that my heart feels warm just from looking at them and being in their presence, but is that enough?

I'm only just finding myself after getting lost in one complicated and dysfunctional relationship. If I struggled to keep hold of my dreams and goals and what makes me the person I am with just one man, how would I cope with three? I trust them more than it should be possible to trust anyone after such a short space of time, but that doesn't mean I can trust myself. And there's a big risk that they'll swamp me without even knowing. It's inevitable with three such big, strong men with big hearts and big personalities.

I'm lost in my thoughts when Max scoops me up and tosses me over his shoulder. Did he notice my hesitation and wants to break the silence, or is he oblivious to the conflict raging inside me? "I think it's time for the eating part of today," he laughs. "I'm hungry as a beast."

"Sounds good," Mason says as I slap Max's back and squeal for him to put me down.

"What are you going to give me if I do?" he teases.

"A kiss," I say.

"Not good enough." Max strides forward until we're on the sand, heading back to the sun loungers.

"A blow job," I laugh, swatting him again, my stomach beginning to hurt where it's pressed against his strong shoulder.

He drops me down to my feet and grabs my face in his hands, planting a kiss on my lips. "That's more like it.

First, eat. You're going to need your strength for what we have in store for you."

I beam, but behind the smile, all I can think is that I am going to need strength. Strength to live in the moment and strength to realize when the moment is over, and it will have to be soon because Mom and Conrad are due back tomorrow.

# 22

Lunch is delivered to the beach; towering club sandwiches, and Long Island iced tea. Miller insists I try his favorite meal, and I'm glad I agree. The drink is refreshing and makes my head swim in the best possible way.

We play a few rounds of poker, which the boys suggest should involve stripping, but then I point out that I'm only wearing two clothing items, and they are only wearing one. We'd be naked in a second, which was probably their aim, but maybe not the most sensible thing we could do in the open air.

We play some paddleball too, but the boys are too good for me, and I end up running for the missed balls so much that I'm exhausted after ten minutes. As I gulp down half a bottle of chilled water, Miller moves closer. He takes my bottle and drinks too, and then he presses his cold lips against mine.

"You really are the sexiest woman," he says.

"Isn't she…" Max says, coming closer behind me until I can feel the warmth of his chest against my back.

Mason's there too, his hand smoothing my windswept hair behind my ear in the way that I love, and suddenly I'm surrounded by my boys.

My boys.

Even as I think it, I glance around at their gorgeous faces. I know what they want, to lose themselves in me while I lose myself in them. We're all looking for that comfort…that oblivion, and I know they can take me higher than I've ever gone before.

We're out in the open, but I don't care. I'm practically vibrating with want, trembling with need.

If Miller slid his fingers down the front of my very skimpy swimsuit, he'd slip right through my pussy. He'd need tissues to wipe away my arousal from his hand.

I'm not really expecting him to do what I just imagined, but he does. Not before he whispers in my ear that he wants to touch me, and would that be okay?

I don't think there has ever been a more rushed, more breathlessly gasped "yes" in the history of positive responses.

Mason moves closer, and hands graze over the skin of my arms and belly, setting all my nerve endings tingling as Miller's finger finds my clit. When he does, he doesn't move; he just holds that finger at a medium pressure that is pure torture when added to everything else that his brothers are doing.

"She's wet," Miller murmurs.

"Of course she is," Mason says, his palm grazing my erect nipple just enough to make me fizz.

Max presses his cock harder against my ass. "How easy would it be for me to bend her over right now and push inside that hot, slippery pussy?"

Miller's fingers find my entrance, and he pushes at least two of them deep inside me until I'm rising up on my tiptoes with the sensation. "Very easy," Miller says. "In fact…" He pushes in another finger and twists his hand until I make an animalistic grunting sound. "I think we could both push in pretty easy. I think Natalie would like that."

"Would you like that, Natalie?"

"Yes," I gasp.

Miller kisses my mouth, his tongue sliding against mine as his fingers move inside me. He pulls back, gently turning my head, so I'm facing Mason who kisses me too; different but so much the same. Where's Max? I turn to pull him to my right side so that I can kiss him too.

Three men.

Three whole individuals but three parts of something that feels like one to me. There's a unity about them. A wholeness that doesn't make sense but feels completely natural.

"Take me inside," I say.

Miller eases his hand from inside me, bringing his fingers to his lips. "You taste so sweet," he says.

"She does," Mason agrees.

I close my eyes, the energy between us so overwhelming that I don't know how I'm going to make it all the way back to the house without my knees collapsing.

A phone rings, and it's a distant sound. "Is that yours?" Max asks. He reaches to where my beach bag is resting on the sun lounger. The handle vibrates as I rummage around to find it.

Nate.

I don't want to accept the call after what happened last time, so I stand staring at the screen while it rings and rings and rings. Why does he not understand that it's over? Why is he harassing me like this?

"Give it to me," Max says, his hand outreached.

"If you shout at him, it will only make things worse."

"Worse than this?" Mason rests his hand on my lower back. "Your hands are shaking."

The phone stops ringing, and the screen goes black. Maybe that'll be it. Maybe I can keep ignoring him until he gets the message. He's miles away, and he's going to get bored. He has all those other girls at his disposal – women who hear about his blog's popularity and want to be a part of it. I'm about to shove the phone back into my bag when it beeps that I've received a message.

"Is it him?" Mason asks.

"I don't want to look," I say. "Here." When I hand the phone to Max, he goes straight to my messages. When he swears under his breath and starts to look around, my heart starts to race. "What is it?"

"He's here. He's fucking here?"

Max thrusts the phone into Mason's hand, and when he presses to watch the video message, I see what's gotten Max so riled up. It's a video of us taken seconds before. A video of me kissing my three stepbrothers one after the other, clear enough that you can see precisely what Miller's hand is doing between my legs. I glance around, as Max starts jogging up the beach toward the house. That's where the video was taken from.

Mason and Miller chase their brother, bare feet kicking up sand as they run, and I follow, knowing that this could get bad so quickly. It's bad already. Nate has a blog with over a million followers. If he uploads that video and tags me in it, everyone will know. Mom will find out. Conrad will see what his sons have been doing to his stepdaughter. Everyone will be disgusted and my career will be over.

Who will want my name listed on their work? Businesses don't want scandal like this, and forget me being able to find even basic work. No one will want a slut photographing their wedding or bar mitzvah. I'll be a pariah. A laughing-stock.

I hear the moment that Max catches up to whoever has been lurking in the shadows. I can't make out the shouting at first, and then, when I'm close enough, I see the outline of Nate. Max has him grasped by the front of his shirt, but far from looking scared, Nate looks manic. His eyes are wide, and his mouth is fixed into an unnerving grin that doesn't fit with the threat or gravity of the situation.

"Did you like the video?" Nate says.

"What the fuck are you doing here?" Max bellows. "This is private property. You're trespassing and harassing Natalie."

"Natalie is my girlfriend," Nate says calmly. "I'm here to visit her. It seems that I arrived just in time. It looked very much as though she was being molested out there. Forced to do things that she would never agree to do. If you don't let go of me, I'll call the police and report the assault." His head pivots to find me where I'm wheezing behind Miller and Mason. "Natalie. Are you okay? Get away from them before they hurt you anymore."

"Nate, you don't have to do this."

"Do what? Come and make sure my girlfriend is okay? You left in such a hurry and with no explanation. I've been so worried, and it seems my worries were justified. It's okay, though. I have it all on video, which can be used as evidence." He puts his hands onto Max's and tries to pull them apart to free himself, but Max is glowering down at him, unyielding.

"You're sick in the head," Max hisses. "Spying on people, making videos."

"I'm sick? Says the man who was forcing a poor helpless girl to do things with his brothers. What kind of arrangement do you have going on? Using the brute force of three against one weak woman?"

Max starts to shove Nate backward toward the trunk of a large palm. Nate's feet scuttle as he struggles to keep himself upright. "You listen to me, you fucking piece of shit. You're delusional. Your behavior is disturbed. You're trespassing and spying, and I'm sure the police would be very interested to see the evidence of that on your phone." Max uses a hand to search Nate's pocket, pulling out his phone and tossing it to Mason. "Find the video," he says. "Delete it from the message app and the gallery. Check to see if his phone is cloud linked and delete it from there too."

I watch as Mason flicks through multiple screens, following Max's instructions. When I glance up at Nate, he's still smiling, and I don't get it. Why isn't he disappointed that the evidence he was so gleeful to have in his possession is being quickly erased?

"It's done," Mason says, tossing the phone back to Max who leans in close to Nate's face.

"Now you listen, and you listen good. If I ever see you at his house again, I'll have you arrested. If you ever call Natalie again, I'll report you for harassment. You're not going to call her, email her, message her, contact her through social media. No fucking letters or getting friends to contact her either. You're going to walk away from his house and accept that she doesn't want you anymore. Do you understand me?"

Max thrusts Nate back, letting go of his shirt as though he can't bear to touch him any longer. Far from appearing scared or chastened, Nate calmly adjusts his shirt and slides his phone back into his pocket.

"Natalie," he says slowly. "I know this isn't you. You need to get away from here, away from these men, before they really hurt you. I can help you. I can get you the medical assistance you need."

"She doesn't need medical assistance. She doesn't need your assistance with anything," Miller shouts. Mason puts his hand on Miller's shoulder.

"You need to leave, right now," Mason says calmly.

Maybe it's the calmness in his voice that makes Nate realize that it's time to go. Or maybe it's because he's had his fun. There's something wrong about this situation where, despite my stepbrothers holding the position of physical power, Nate still appears to think he's the puppet master. He walks around Max and heads in the direction of the beach, probably the way he came in. Max, Mason, and Miller follow him, watching for a long time as he saunters down the beach as though he's on a pleasurable stroll, not leaving the scene of an altercation.

Mason is the first to turn, finding me standing a few feet behind. He's the first to pull me into a fierce hug. My arms hang limply at my sides. My mind seems stuck, the shock of what just happened leaving me fractured. "You're okay," Mason says. "We will never let anyone hurt you, do you understand?"

Miller rests his hand on my back, and so does Max. "He's gone," Max says. "You don't have to worry. He's not going to be coming back."

"He will," I say. The words leave my lips slowly and calmly, but inside I feel anything but. Maybe they didn't see Nate's half-smile or understand that his swagger is based on the fact that he has a plan that he hasn't yet revealed. He's holding the trump card, but they think they've scared him away.

"I deal with assholes like him day in day out," Max says. "Trust me."

I could tell Max all of my fears, but it's not going to make any difference. What can we do? Reporting Nate for trespassing won't be taken seriously. We were in a relationship last week. He will say he was here to reconcile. The police will let him go, and he'll be angrier than ever. Showing the boys that I'm scared isn't going to help either. I don't want to put them at risk by making them angry. What if they go looking for him to threaten him again? He could accuse them of harassment. He could ruin their lives.

Best to keep to the plan. Ignore Nate, hope for the best, and pray.

# 23

That night we don't have sex. I guess the boys know that what happened with Nate has left me feeling too traumatized and vulnerable. I need them for the reassurance that comes with cuddles and kisses, and sleeping with them surrounding me. Max suggests we use the spare room with the largest bed, which is perfect for all of us.

I don't cry, even though I feel the tears burning in my throat. We don't talk about what happened either, and I guess they can sense how close I am to breaking down. They don't want to push me there. They must talk about what happened when I'm in the shower, and if they've formulated any kind of plan about it, they don't share it with me. I'm glad about that. It'd only make me feel awkward and more upset than I already am.

Maybe I'm guilty of burying my head in the sand. Perhaps we should be more transparent about what's happened, but then again, this can only be a short-lived fantasy for all of us. I have to be strong about that because I don't think Mason, Miller, and Max will be. As they sleep around me, content and peaceful, I see how happy they are in this crazy arrangement. I wonder if being triplets is a bit like being part of one of those toddler puzzles with only three pieces. Apart, their picture is still clear enough to be made out but it's only when they're put together that you see the image in all its glory.

I don't sleep well, drifting in and out of disturbingly vivid dreams that only exacerbate the sick feeling I have in my belly. Nate came back to get me. He interrupted his itinerary to seek me out, and the things he was saying were even stranger than in Thailand. For the first time, I really consider whether his mental state is where it should be. Is he aware of his lies and manipulation, or is he delusional? I'm not sure which is scarier.

At some time before dawn, I stir, finding lips kissing my neck and hands caressing my belly and my legs. It's so warm in the room, and I'm existing halfway between sleep and consciousness as someone parts my legs and slides his tongue over my clit. More warmth as lips find my nipple, sucking gently. More heat as a mouth finds mine and kisses hot, wet, and deep. I don't open my eyes to find out who is where. It doesn't really matter. All I know is that my stepbrothers are making me feel good. They're making me forget, and I won't stop them.

For now, they own me.

I'm too weak to resist. Too weak to tell them this is wrong when everything about it feels so right. I succumb to it all – the pleasure and the pain – hoping that in the morning I can find a way to be stronger and for everything to go back to the way it should be.

My heart can't take any more fractures.

And most of all, I don't want these amazing men to suffer because I can't seem to help but make bad decisions.

# 24

I'm the first to wake, slipping out of bed to sit on the balcony overlooking the sea. It's rougher today, surging with white foam-topped waves that appear with sudden anger, run their course, and subside into the sea's depths.

When Mom researched our family tree, she found our ancestral roots in a small fishing village in Ireland. Many men of our line had spent their lives at the mercy of the world's surging waters, and many had died. It made me wonder if maybe there is something in my blood that draws me to look upon the might of the very thing that was such a danger to my ancestors. Maybe it's the same fathomless might that drew them to risk their lives. The bond between fisherman and ocean is complex, a love/hate obsession that takes them back to the deep over and over, despite the risks.

The heart is that way too, love a siren's song that tempts us despite the dangers.

The darker waters before me seem somehow prophetic. Yesterday, until Nate appeared, all was calm, but now his actions have disturbed everything. In the bedroom, Mason,

Miller, and Max sleep, and all I want to do is curl up with them under the pure white cotton sheet and let the rest of the world disappear. I could take a deep breath and slip beneath the waves, drifting down and down and down until I'm lost to everything that came before. But if I do that, will I lose myself again? Will I drown in a situation that holds so many difficulties in its grasp?

Can I be the woman who trusts three men, where trusting one has brought me so much hardship?

Can I be the woman who fights for an uncertain love, harming others in the process?

Max turned off my phone last night, but I power it on so that I can speak with Connie. I need her friendship to pull me to shore. She'll hear me and give me good advice. I know she will.

Friends are like our anchors. They allow us our freedom to roam but can reach out to fix us in place for our own good if we need them too. This feels like one of those times.

I dial her number, and she picks up almost immediately, sounding sleepy.

"Hey, I was just about to get up. Are you okay?"

"I don't think I am," I say softly.

I can hear the rustle of sheets as Connie moves to sit. "Tell me what's going on."

"Nate was here yesterday. He's been calling and messaging, but he just showed up without any notice."

"Shit. I had a feeling he would."

"Did you really? I thought he'd have more pride."

Connie clears her throat to get rid of the sleepy croakiness. "He has enough of a fucked-up ego to think he could come back and get you to change your mind. He can't accept that you'd reject him. He doesn't want other people to see that he's not the perfect boyfriend. That's enough pressure to get him on that flight. So what did you say to him?"

I take a deep breath, the memory of yesterday's confrontation bringing back the surge of panic I felt when I received the video message.

"He saw me with…my stepbrothers, and he recorded us."

There's a pause as Connie digests. She knew about Mason but not about the others. For all her encouragement, I don't think she would have believed I would have gone through with forming my very own harem in a million years. The Natalie she knows would have run a mile from that kind of situation, too shy and repressed to even consider it. "What were you doing with them? What did Nate record?"

"I was kissing them, and they were touching me."

"Where? As in the location?" she adds quickly.

"The private beach where the house is."

"Shit." Connie's sheets rustle again, and I hear the thump of her feet on the wooden floor of her apartment. "And Nate sent you the video?"

"He sent it to me, but the boys made sure it was deleted from his phone."

"Did he send it to anyone else?"

"I don't think so."

"Okay. That's good. What did Nate say?"

"He told me he would help me report my stepbrothers to the police for molesting me."

"WHAT?"

"I know. I really don't get it. I don't understand his train of thought. It was pretty damned obvious I wasn't struggling and that everything that was happening was consensual."

"This probably isn't the right time for me to say this, but I'm so jealous I'm the color of a fucking lime right now."

"Yeah, not the right time," I say, smiling through my misery.

"Okay, I'll let it go, but at some time in the future when you're not dealing with a psycho, please tell me all the juicy bits. Everything. Let me live vicariously through your amazing life. Nothing is TMI."

"I'm making no promises," I say, imagining Connie's scowling face.

"So, what are you going to do?"

I sigh, resting my cheek in my palm. "I have no idea. I have three gorgeous, amazing men sleeping ten feet away who are so good to me it's practically obscene, and a deranged ex who is trying to mess up my life. It's like a giant house of cards in the path of a typhoon."

Connie's coffee machine starts up in the background, and I glance at my watch, realizing that she'll need to get ready soon or risk being late for work. "The three men don't seem to be the problem, then?"

"Three men is three times the problem, Connie. Three times the risk of heartbreak for all of us."

"You can't go into relationships thinking about heartbreak," Connie says. "You're dooming things before they even have a chance."

"But just plowing headlong into foolishness isn't ideal either. I mean, whoever heard of a successful relationship between one woman and three men?"

"Me," Connie says. "Do you know how many people are living that lifestyle? Maybe it's a natural progression of women's sexual liberation, or maybe it's to do with all the economic pressures out there. Raising a family with one breadwinner isn't always an option these days, but add two more men into the mix, and you have a household that's swimming with cash."

"Swimming with dick too," I say, shocking myself at my vulgarity.

Connie snorts with laughter. "Money and dick…it's a perfect combination."

We chuckle for a while, and I shake my head. "What the hell am I going to do, Con? I can't live this life. I'm not a trailblazer for the women's lib movement. I'm just an ordinary girl who needs to live an ordinary life."

"See, that's where you're getting everything mixed up. There's nothing ordinary about you. You're extraordinary, and that's why you have three sex gods on their knees, ready to worship you. They see in you what you don't see yourself."

"I don't think so."

"You need to wake up and see how amazing you are and then believe it deep in your heart. If you can't see it, how will you ever allow someone else to love you the way that you deserve? This is why you accepted Nate. It's because you didn't believe that you deserved any better than him, and that is just sad, Natalie. It's really sad."

"I don't want to be the thing they use to indulge their kink," I say, trying to deflect away from Connie's analysis. The truth is so hard to hear when it strips you bare.

"Is that what you really believe they want you for? To fulfill a kink? Don't you think they could look for someone outside their home for that? Someone who's not going to be around once they're bored and moving on. Men don't like to shit where they eat, Natalie. The fact that they're pursuing you despite the risk tells me a whole lot about them. The fact that they've jumped in to save your ass with Nate too. If they didn't care, they wouldn't bother. They'd leave you to deal with it, or use it as an excuse to kick you to the curb."

I'm silent as I digest, and Connie gives me the space to think, stirring her three sugars into her black coffee. A lot of what she's saying makes sense, but that doesn't make it easier for me to accept. Is it worse to believe that they actually feel something for me outside the sexual attraction? Is it worse to believe that this really is the lifestyle they want to lead in the long term?

What Connie said about me is right. I've never had the confidence that is needed to be able to find the right relationship or to push myself in my career. I've just stumbled around, getting swept up or guided by other people. When was the last time I really thought about what I want in the long term and actively took steps toward it? I don't think I ever have. It's hard to admit that to myself that I've drifted and hard to know what to do with the information. Soul searching takes time. Defining a plan past next week takes real, considered thought. It takes the ability to decide between options and to take risks.

All of that scares the shit out of me.

I hear Connie take a tentative sip of her coffee. "You know, in the end, all you have to do is talk. Explain how you feel. Ask them how they feel. We all spend so much time messing around with imagining what the other person is thinking rather than just being upfront. We worry about scaring people away, but if someone is that easily frightened, then we're better off without them. Just be honest."

"I guess," I say, already feeling panic surging at the very thought of opening up. It seems easier to hold myself as tight as a clamshell. It seems easier to run than face the music. "But what if I don't know how I feel? What if I don't know what I want? What if I can't ever seem to make a confident decision either way?"

"Then you'll drift. It's not always a bad thing. Sometimes people end up stumbling into their best life. Fate, or whatever. Maybe that's what's happening here. Nate showed his true colors, you returned home, and now you're sharing a bed with three hotties. I mean, you couldn't have done better if you'd planned and schemed, could you?"

I gaze over my shoulder to where Miller and Max are sleeping, and Mason is stirring. Connie is right. I have stumbled into a piece of heaven that I could never have even imagined, let alone set as a life goal. But allowing myself to keep stumbling forward is harder, especially when I know that this could be bad for us all.

Turning back, the sea swells before me. Angry and tempestuous. A warning.

Sheets rustle and feet thud on the floor in the bedroom. Mason is up, and I need to finish this conversation. "I have to go, Connie."

"Of course you do. You have three men to satisfy. Woe is you." She makes a disgusted sound and then chuckles to herself. "Call me whenever you need to, especially if anything else happens with Nate. Let me at him, and I'll fuck him up for you with my bare hands."

She probably would as well, such is Connie's ferocious loyalty.

"I will. I'm sorry, and I love you."

I hang up just as Mason steps out onto the balcony. "Hey," I say softly. "Sorry if I disturbed you."

His hair is messy from sleep, but it only seems to make him sexier. His eyes squint from the brightness of the sun. Something about the way he looks at me is different. There's a coolness in the blue of his gaze that wasn't there before. Like the sea, today, something has changed. Maybe it was seeing me with Nate and knowing the kind of man I'd linked myself to before. Some men are jealous that way. They don't want to know that you have a sexual history. They certainly don't want to be able to picture the ex. "I'm going to go down to my room," he says. "Get showered, and then I'm going to be out for the day."

"Okay," I say, expecting him to tell me where he's going and kiss me, but he doesn't do either. There's just a pause where that kiss should be. When his eyes scan over me, his face impassively drifts to face the sea. I want to ask him if he feels the same way I do, that this thing could really be something good between us, but the words remain trapped in my mind, fixed there by too many years of being a coward. Then he steps back into the room and turns to leave.

I watch him walk away, taking with him any confidence I had that what happened between us was about anything more than sex. I'm experienced enough to know a brush-off when I feel one.

Fuck.

I'm a fool to believe that they cared about me even a little, and now that things are getting complicated they're going to drop me like a hot brick. Maybe it would have lasted longer if Nate hadn't appeared, but now my situation is too much hassle. This is exactly why I kept telling myself that letting go of my inhibitions was a bad idea. There's an ache in my chest that shouldn't be there. I shouldn't feel anything for these men, and it definitely shouldn't bother me that this is coming to an end.

But it does, and I'm so angry with myself.

Connie was right. I need to focus on my long-term plan, not mess around making things complicated. I need to focus on me and what I'm going to do with my life. If I do that, I can get out of this house and leave this uncomfortable situation behind. Then Nate won't know where to find me either. It's the solution to all my problems.

Except none of it will erase the ache in my heart at the thought of never being held by the Banbury triplets again.

But even that will pass in time, as the saying goes.

I'll heal and move on. I'll do what I planned and shut myself off.

I'll find a way to be happy without Mason, Max, and Miller.

And everything will be okay.

A tear rolls down my cheek, and I swipe it angrily because all my internal reassurance hasn't convinced my heart. Then I clasp my phone in my hand and stand, taking a shaky breath as I walk past Miller and Max, who are still sleeping.

Today is a new day, and I'm back where I started.

Alone.

# 25

I call down to have breakfast bought to my room. It feels crazy to have room service in my own home, but it's not going to be for long. I shower and dress quickly, and now I'm running searches for photography jobs, desperately seeking something that could set me free.

I'm searching right across the country because being near home isn't going to fix anything. A fresh start is what's going to make everything better. As I review a job that is based in New York, my throat burns. You're running away, my mind whispers traitorously.

Coward.

I think about calling Connie again, but I don't know what I'd say.

And I know she's only going to tell me more of what I can't bear to hear.

The thing is, all my searching is really in vain because my portfolio isn't up to date. I need to spend time editing shots and loading them onto my website. It's time I don't have. I click away from the job search, flicking through the folders on my laptop, thinking about which images I could improve quickly. There are some from Mexico and Brazil that I spent time on for Nate's blog. They were good enough. As I'm scrolling, the folder from the recent book cover shoot jumps out at me.

Mason and Miller.

The images I took of them are nothing like the other shots in my gallery. Maybe it'd be good to use some of them to show my repertoire and versatility. I could choose a few of the best ones and work on them. They'd grab attention if nothing else.

I click on some of the last images I took of Miller naked. As the picture enlarges on my screen, my breath hitches. His eyes stare out as though they're looking directly at me, as though they're seeing into my soul.

I remember how it felt to take the photos. The way my pulse raced. The heat all over my body. The wetness between my legs. I remember how much I wanted him, well, wanted Mason. The memory feels tangled and twisted, the real and the imagined all blurred into one.

I start to make small alterations, cropping, and enhancing the lighting. I'm engrossed in the image, engrossed in the fantasy that Miller spun that day. When there's a knock at my door, I don't think quickly enough to close the image down, and when I turn, Mom is there looking straight at the screen. Straight at the practically pornographic photo of her stepson.

"Natalie," she gasps. "What have you done?"

"Mom." I stand quickly so that my body is blocking the image from view, but it's too late. Mom doesn't know anything about the photoshoot. She doesn't know I was paid to photograph Conrad's sons and that it was all a coincidence. She must be thinking the worst. "How was your trip?"

Mom's hands twist together, always so expressive of her mood. "What have you done?" she says again through gritted teeth, her eyes widening with every word.

"It was a job," I say. "For a publishing company."

Mom blinks, her brow folding into a confused frown. "What was?"

"The photo." I step back, waving to Miller on the screen, and Mom's hand rushes to cover her mouth in shock.

"You took that photo of your stepbrother? Why would you do that?"

"It was a job. Connie found it for me. I didn't know who Mason was, not until we met at the front door the day after."

Mom blinks slowly, her hand still clasped to her face. "And the video?" she says. "The video Nate sent me. What was that?"

I take a step back, recalling Nate's smile as Mason was deleting the images. Now I understand his smugness. He'd already sent the video to Mom. He'd already sealed my fate.

"How could you?" she says with genuine pain in her voice. "How could you? This is my marriage. My family. Your family. How could you do that…with three men…with your stepbrothers?"

"I didn't know who Mason was," I say. "We…" I don't know how to tell my mom that I jumped into bed with a man after meeting him a few hours earlier. Some things aren't meant to be shared with parents.

"You slept with him after taking his photos," Mom says, her voice rising with each word. "And then what? Moved onto his brother's. Three of them. All three of them." She's practically squeaking at this point, and I have no idea what to say. "Is this why you broke up with Nate? Because you were unfaithful. He's devastated about it, Natalie. You've broken his heart. And you've broken mine."

Her voice hitches on the last word, and she turns and leaves the room. I don't stop her. What's the point of correcting her about Nate when it's the rest that she's really disappointed about? I can't blame her for how she feels, either.

A mistake is a mistake.

I turn back to the image on the screen, and Miller gazes back at me.

The one time I gave in to my desires and took charge has brought everything crashing down around me.

There's only one thing left for me to do.

Finding Connie's number in my phone, I call and ask for a favor.

# 26

"It'll only be for a few days," I tell Connie as she passes me a bundle of sheets and pillows for the pullout bed in her living room, which is also her kitchen and dining space. She rents a tiny apartment, and I feel awful for asking to stay with her, but I don't have a choice. There's no way I could hang around at the beach house knowing how Mom feels about what happened between my stepbrothers and me, and no way I wanted to face Mason, Miller, and Max so they could brush me off.

I left as soon as I could pack my things. I hadn't fully unpacked my suitcase, so it was easy to scoop up my life and transfer it here.

"You don't have to worry about anything," Connie says. "You're welcome to stay."

"But, it's not exactly ideal to have me sleeping in your only reception room."

"It's fine. I'm glad you called, and I'm happy to be your escape route. Your mom sounded like she was on the warpath. Sometimes it's best to get out before you both end up saying things you don't mean."

"She made her feelings quite clear, and I can't say I blame her. This whole situation was ridiculous from the start."

"From what you've told me, I don't get the sudden switch with Mason. One second they're stepping in to manhandle Nate and telling you they want you and then next he's blowing cold. It doesn't make any sense."

"It doesn't need to," I say, pulling the lever to flip the sofa into a bed. "Even if they were down on their knees with a ring, my mom and Conrad wouldn't give their blessing."

Connie shrugs. "Love is worth fighting for, no matter the barriers. But that's not the situation you're in, so no point in talking about it." She tosses me the sheet, and I shake it out over the mattress. We work together, folding the corners and tucking in both sides. I'm pretty sure this bed is going to be very uncomfortable, but beggars can't be choosers.

"Did I tell you that I've sent my résumé for a job in New York?"

"New York. So far…" She tosses a pillow at me and screws up her face. "You've only just got back, and now you're running off again."

"I haven't got the position yet. They might not even want to interview me."

"Again, with the negativity. Seriously, Natalie. When they see your stuff, they're going to be begging for you to relocate."

"That is what I'm hoping for. I need to get away from here. A fresh start."

"The grass always seems greener." Connie perches on the edge of the bed and looks at her nails. "You think I haven't thought about giving up my life here and starting somewhere new?"

"Why haven't you?"

"Because I know that I'll just be taking my problems with me. A new job and a new home doesn't necessarily bring new happiness. I need to focus on sorting my shit out here."

"What shit do you have to sort out?" I ask, feeling suddenly very guilty. Since I got back, all I've done is go on about my problems and my issues. I've leaned so hard on my friend that her back is practically folded in two, and what have I found out about her? I've been away for nearly a year. So much must have happened that I don't know about.

"It doesn't matter. Nothing major."

"No, seriously. Talk to me." I sit next to her and angle my body so I'm giving her my full attention. I guess it will have to be better late than never.

"Well, my job isn't really turning out as I hoped. They sold me with the prospect of promotion, but I'm still stuck doing the same thing after two years. All that time at college and I could have gotten this job straight out of high school. This place isn't exactly my dream home." She waves her hand around the tiny space. She's done a lot to make it nice, but it's very basic. "And I haven't had a serious relationship in over a year. This just isn't what I imagined my twenties would be like."

"I know what you mean," I say. "In the movies, everyone is living in huge loft apartments with streams of sexy guys and dream jobs. They're selling us a lie."

"And we fall for it, hook, line, and sinker."

I shrug. "Maybe you should be looking for a new job in New York too. We could move there together. Start over on some greener grass. Take a chance."

Connie smiles and shrugs. "I guess I wouldn't lose anything."

"Exactly."

"Okay. Tomorrow I'll start checking out the online job sites."

I clap my hands, trying to be excited at the prospect of doing something that will potentially help Connie as much as it helps me, but I feel different on the inside. My heart doesn't want to run. It wants Mason, Miller, and Max to tell me that they can't live without me. It wants a life with them and everything that life will bring: love and laughter, warmth and comfort, passion, and fulfillment.

I want all of those things for my friend too.

But it isn't my destiny. Everything that has happened over the past week has been just a stepping stone on my journey, and maybe this job, if I get it, will be another stone. Who knows where my path will lead?

My phone pings, and I reach for it as Connie stretches and then goes to fix us both a glass of water. It's a message from Beresford. My heart speeds as I open the email and quickly scan his words. "Thank you for sending the photographs. I think the paintings are really fresh and interesting. I'd be very interested in seeing them in person and anything else the artist has. How about next week?"

Next week.

He must really like them to free up time in his diary so soon.

This is Mason's big chance, but with things as they are between us, I don't know what to do. I'll sound like a weirdo stalker if I call him and tell him I took photographs of his paintings without him knowing, and I'll sound even worse for sending them to a gallery behind his back. It was supposed to be a great surprise, and it would have been if things hadn't turned out so awkwardly.

I tell Connie about the messages and show her the images of Mason's paintings. "Wow," she says. "I can see why you wanted to get these looked at by someone in the industry. They're amazing."

"I know, but how do I tell Mason about this? I really don't want to have to talk to him, and I'm worried about appearing to be a desperate tryhard."

"I get it. It's not exactly a straightforward situation."

"But if I don't tell him, it feels mean."

"You have to tell him. It's…just how." Connie strokes her chin like a mad Bond villain trying to develop a plan to take over the world. "I think this is one we need to sleep on."

"Yeah, sorry. It's so late, and you have work tomorrow."

She waves as though my concerns are misplaced. "We'll work it all out," she says. "But maybe two fresh minds, a pot of coffee and some donuts, we might get to a better answer."

"Okay, goodnight, and thanks again."

"Say thanks one more time, and I'll put laxative in your coffee in the morning." Connie grins devilishly, and I'm pretty certain that it's not an idle threat.

"Okay. Goodnight."

When she's slipped off to her room, I pull up my phone again. Just as I'm searching through to find Beresford's email again, the screen lights up.

Mason.

I watch as it silently rings, his name emblazoned across my screen in the same way it feels etched across my heart. Why is he calling? Maybe to tell me how much my mom raged at them for having sex with me. If that happened, it would be completely mortifying.

I can't deal with this now. There's just been too much going on in my life in such a short space of time. Hearing his voice will only bring back everything that I feel for him and his brothers. It'll reopen the wound I've been trying and failing to bandage.

It rings for a long time, and I watch, feeling a tiny connection to a man who seems so far away now. While he's calling me, it's as though he's reaching out to take my hand. If I don't pick up, I'll never know that he was really calling to get angry with me for putting them all in an awkward position. I can pretend it's something different, and that just makes it easier.

I'll deal with Beresford's email tomorrow. Sometimes sleep helps to sort out the tangled mess of our thoughts, and if not, I'll let Connie decide what to do next.

# 27

"I've been thinking about the painting problem. Why don't you ask Beresford to contact Mason directly? He doesn't have to disclose who sent the pictures. He'll never have to know it was you," Connie says, chewing on a mouthful of granola.

"That's actually not a bad idea." I pour a steaming cup of coffee, hoping that it's going to wake me up. I slept terribly last night, with too much on my mind to truly rest. That, and Connie's sofa bed has definitely seen better days, or too many active nights.

"So what are you going to do after that?"

"More job hunting," I say.

"In New York?"

"I think so…basically anywhere that is far away from here."

Connie sips her coffee. "Far away from here would be good. If you get time, do some searching for me too. I'll send you my résumé. You can send it into anything you think would be good for me."

"Sure."

Connie rises, gripping the side of her empty bowl and carrying it to the sink. "And what about Nate? If he calls again?"

"I'm not picking up."

"Good. But I'm worried about that douchebag being persistent."

"I'm really not sure what's going to happen. He twisted things around so that my mom thinks it was me who was unfaithful. She actually sided with him."

"Well, your mom should believe in you way more than she actually does. That's a conversation you're going to need to have at some point."

"Great. I think moving might just be easier."

Connie grins, reaching for her lunchbox. "It definitely would be, but we're too old to be burying our problems."

"I'm absolutely fine with burying mine and hoping that they never rise again."

"Like Nate…that went really well!"

"Not like Nate."

"So, I'll see you later. Good luck!" Connie breezes out of the apartment, clutching her purse and lunch, and takes with her everything that was keeping me buoyant. It's easy to keep smiling when my bestie is distracting me, but now I'm alone, that heartache slides back in. I wonder what Mason, Miller, and Max are doing right now. Are they seducing their next conquest? Maybe they've already gotten her into bed. Maybe they're doing all the amazing things to her that they did to me. I shiver, remembering the kisses on my spine, the slide of tongues between my legs, the press of a cock at my opening. I groan aloud, recalling the feeling of security I had lying between them.

There isn't even a part of me that is hurting because of Nate anymore. All the longing and aching is for my stepbrothers and it's totally pointless to feel this way.

It was never going to work.

I have to accept that and move on, just like I did with Nate.

My laptop is resting on the table and I slide it in front of me, taking a deep breath before opening it up. As I start to search for a job that will take me far away from the men who've stolen my heart, everything seems grayer. Rather than excitement, I feel dread uncoiling in my belly.

I switch to my email, opening the one from Beresford and replying to him as Connie suggested. When I click send, it feels like another nail in the coffin enclosing my hopes and dreams. It was the one reason I had to get in touch with Mason, and I've given it away.

Beresford replies almost immediately, thanking me for the lead and a bright feeling of pride wells up inside me. If this is Mason's big break, and he eventually finds out it was me who promoted his work, he won't be able to forget me. Something good will come from all this. I stand, closing the computer and stomp off to take a shower. I scrub my skin with frustration, emerging pink and slightly sore. Just as I'm pulling on my leggings and racer-back workout top, my phone rings.

Nate, I think. Or Mom. Or one of my gorgeous stepbrothers. They all run through my head as I dash to the table to retrieve my phone. Instead, it's a number I don't recognize.

"Hello."

"Hi, is that Natalie Monk?"

"It is. Who is this?"

"Hi Natalie, my name is Robert Hunter. I'm the recruiter for Eco-soldiers, a charity that is fighting to save endangered habitats around the world."

"I'm afraid I can't make a contribution," I say, feeling flustered.

"No." I can hear the smile in his voice. "I'm calling because we're looking for a photographer to document our most recent achievements and when we saw your portfolio…well, you seem perfect for the role."

"You saw my portfolio?"

"Well, we were introduced to you by Mason Banbury. He's been a supporter for a number of years and knew we had a position open. He speaks very highly of you, Natalie. We'd love for you to come and meet with us to go through the role. If you're interested, and the terms meet your requirements, I think you could be a really great addition to our team."

Mason recommended me for a job. I don't get it at all. He seemed to want to get rid of me, to brush what we did under the carpet. Why would he be bothered to help me find a job?

"I'd…well, I'd love to come and find out more about the role," I say.

"Today?" Robert says.

"I could today," I say, glancing down at my casual clothes, mind already spinning through the contents of my suitcase for a suitable outfit. I'll have to make my own way. There's no driver waiting conveniently outside Connie's modest home.

"That would be fantastic. I have your email address. I'll send through details. Would twelve pm work for you?"

"Yes. That would be fine."

"Okay great. We'll see you then."

There's a click on the other end of the line as Robert hangs up and I stare at the phone as though I've suddenly discovered I'm actually holding a banana. I don't understand what just happened.

My phone pings with the arrival of Robert's email and I scan through the job spec, my heart accelerating with every word. It's a global role involving extensive travel to some of the most breathtaking countries in the world. They're looking for someone with my experience. Someone who can turn landscapes and the natural world into compelling pictorial stories. It's everything that I did for Nate but for a good cause. I learn on their website how much they are doing for species that are on the brink of extinction. Habitat preservation has to be the priority.

This is an amazing opportunity.

I cover my mouth with my hand, totally overwhelmed that Mason suggested me for it. I want to pick up the phone and thank him for his kind recommendation but I can't. His expression on the balcony floods my mind. The flippant way he left me that morning without a kiss. He must have sent the recommendation before that day. It's the only explanation.

It doesn't take me long to get dressed. I grab my laptop and head out into the morning sunshine, a flutter of brightness surging through me.

When I left Nate I didn't dare dream that something like this could happen to me. I envisioned having to take a role that wouldn't fulfill my dreams to continue seeing the world in all of its amazing glory. Now I have a chance.

The little worm of doubt that always wriggles inside me at times like these is there telling me not to get too excited. There's a huge chance that they're not going to like me enough to offer me the role. There is so much I need to ask them about. Maybe the money won't be good. I don't have the luxury of working for nothing anymore. I need to start to build a life for myself and saving is the only way that is going to happen.

I wave for a cab outside Connie's apartment. There is so much traffic on the journey to Eco-soldier's offices that I'm almost late. By the time I arrive, my heart is racing and my palm is slippery around the handle of my purse.

My white palazzo pants cling to my legs and I have to shake out the fabric to make myself presentable. The offices would be ordinary from the outside if it weren't for the spray-painted rainforest that they've commissioned to cover the front of the concrete office block. I love the edginess of the art they've used and the challenging message emblazoned.

I push the heavy metal and glass door open, finding a large colorful reception area. There's a man behind the counter wearing an Eco-soldier t-shirt, complete with logo and camo-style print made out of different leaf designs. He smiles broadly when I approach. "I'm here to meet with Robert Hunter." As I say his name, I register the inappropriateness of his surname for someone working in animal conservation.

"Sure. Take a seat and I'll tell him you're here."

The seats are green metal, not the most comfortable I've ever sat on. I wonder if there's a message in the design. How can we rest comfortably when the world is so full of injustice? My heart is beating too fast and it's making me feel kind of woozy. Not the ideal state of mind when you're about to be interviewed for what could be your dream job. I contemplate pulling my phone from my purse to try to distract myself with something mindless like Facebook but before I have the chance, a man appears from a door at the rear of reception and stalks toward me.

He's tall and blond, a man who could have modeled for a superhero figurine.

"Natalie," he booms, holding out his big hand. "Robert Hunter."

I shuffle to my feet and take his hand, trying to shake it with enough conviction to appear confident. He must be close to six foot seven, so I'm craning my neck.

"Welcome. We really appreciate you coming in with such little notice."

"It's okay," I say. "This is a really exciting opportunity."

"It's awesome you feel that way." He turns, holding his arm out to indicate our direction of passage. "Come this way and we can talk some more."

The next hour goes by in a flash, mainly because I'm so overwhelmed by everything I'm presented with. Robert outlines the charity and its scope and then goes into what they are looking to achieve over the next five years and how the role would fit into that. The more he talks the more I wonder if I'm dreaming. If I could have conjured the most perfect role in the world, I couldn't have done better in my imagination.

When I left Nate, the loss of my dreams, of my future, were so profound it felt like physical pain. Now, listening to Robert, if feels like those dreams are reforming.

I can travel again.

I can take pictures of places that need the world's focus.

I can make a difference.

All of this can only happen if they offer me the job.

I search Robert's face and body language for clues about how positive he feels about me. His body is angled toward me, his eye contact strong and his gesticulating is enthusiastic. My heart skitters faster as hope surges. Could this really happen?

Maybe.

And if it does, it will take me far away from Mason, Max, and Miller.

What happens when your heart wants to pull you in two directions? I guess it breaks into two.

# 28

Life's journey isn't linear. It may seem that way, putting one foot in front of the other, time passing by as we take small steps through our time on earth.

As I walk away from Eco-soldier's offices with a firm and excellent job offer in hand, my gut is telling me that I'm stepping in the wrong direction. My mind, on the other hand, is rationalizing that this is for the best. It finally hit me that my stepbrothers put me forward for this job to get me out of the picture. I'm going to be traveling the world, far away from them. Far away so I won't be able to cause them any more issues. It wasn't about them wanting me to achieve my dreams. Not like when I sent Beresford Mason's paintings. That was selfless. This was selfish.

My cheeks flush hot, and my throat burns.

Stupid girl for thinking anything different. Stupid girl for risking her heart when it was already shattered and drowned in disappointment.

Instead of walking with a spring in my step, my shoulders are slumped, and my gait slow and labored.

Even thoughts of my first assignment, which will be back in Thailand, don't raise my spirits. And to top it all off, I have to tell Connie that our plans to head to New York and start over are on hold for at least twelve months. I know she won't hold it against me. We've been friends for long enough that I know she only ever wants the best for me, but that doesn't stop me from feeling guilty.

What a mess.

I pick up a bottle of wine and some chips for us to share later. A kind of peace offering that feels pathetic and small, but it’s all I can afford.

As I'm turning the corner to Connie's street, I look up and find three familiar-looking figures sitting on the wall outside the door to the building.

The sight of them stops me in my tracks, and it's Max with his eye for trouble who spots my movement from the corner of his eye. When he stands, his brothers stand too, and even from a distance, I can see that their expressions are grave. Has something happened? I realize my phone is still silenced from the interview. Has Mom been in an accident?

They don't move, and I start to feel like a cowboy in a Western, poised to shoot my gun as soon as my opponents draw. I can't just stand here forever, and they're blocking my doorway. With hot shame burning my cheeks, I finally find the strength to propel myself forward.

“Natalie,” Mason says. “How did the interview go?”

He knew about it. I guess Robert must have called him. It’s the only explanation.

“Really good. Thanks for putting me forward.” I cringe at the formality of our exchange. Why does this kind of conversation hurt when you've had someone's face between your legs and their arms wrapped around you?

"That's amazing." Miller reaches out to touch my arm, but I'm not expecting it, and when I flinch, he withdraws his hand quickly with a pained look on his face.

The atmosphere is strained, the triplets glancing at each other and then at me as though they have no idea what to say. I don't either, except to ask the obvious question. "Why are you here?"

"To see you," Max says abruptly. "Shouldn't that be obvious?"

"We should be asking you why you left without saying goodbye…without telling us where you were going or why you felt like you needed to leave so abruptly."

I suck in a sharp breath, the mix of confusion and annoyance in Miller and Max's voice a shock. "Why don't you ask Mason?"

His brother's turn to him and Mason shrugs his shoulders. "I don't know what you're talking about," he says.

I stare at him, trying to figure out if he's telling the truth, but he seems to be genuine. Does he not remember how he brushed me off that morning on the balcony? Was that not his intention? "My mom found out about us, from Nate. Before you got his phone and wiped the video, he sent it to her phone. It was why he was still smiling."

"She confronted you?" Max asks with eyebrows raised.

"She didn't confront you?"

They all shake their heads and I'm confused. Why would Mom be so devastated but not bring it up with my stepbrothers? Maybe she didn't feel like she could approach Conrad's sons that way without telling Conrad. Maybe she's keeping it to herself so as not to rock the boat.

"Why did you think that I knew about this?" Mason asks.

"I didn't," I say. "You...you were really short with me the last time we spoke."

Max and Miller turn to their brother, their faces questioning. "You were talking to someone on the phone," Mason says. "You told them you loved them. I thought you were reconciling with your ex. It was only when Beresford got in touch about my paintings, and you wouldn't pick up, that I got in touch with Connie and found out some of what happened. Your friend is fiercely loyal. It took some serious pleading to get her to spill even a word."

One of Connie's neighbors passes clutching a bag of fast food, and I realize that we must look a little strange having a huge heart-to-heart out in the open like this. "Do you want to come inside?" I ask, hoping they'll say yes and dreading it in equal measure.

My stepbrothers nod in unison and I pass to lead them to Connie's apartment. She's not going to be home for a while, so at the very least, we might be able to part ways without the awkwardness hanging between us. Even as I think it, a rush of hollowness empties out my chest where my heart should be. As they follow me, I feel older and wearier; tired of the loss of love I keep experiencing. My throat burns at the possibility that this could be the last time I see them all for months, even years. Will they walk away once the air between us is cleared? Will they kiss me politely on the cheek and wish me well with my new job? I don't think I could maintain my composure if they did. I don't have that same strength and resolve that I had with Nate.

Mason, Max, and Miller practically fill Connie's small living room. They stand around until I wave my hand toward the sofa. When they take a seat in a row, they remind me of the three wise monkeys. I drop my bags by the wall and lean against the table, not knowing what to do with my hands. They end up clasped in front of me.

"Why didn't you tell us what your mom said?" Miller asks. "We could have supported you. We would have told her how we felt…reassured her. Taken some of the flak, at least."

"I…I just don't want to cause any issues for her, or for you. What would be the point in dragging us all into this mess and creating a huge problem between our parents and between all of us? I left so she wouldn't fear that this would continue under her roof."

"Walking away from difficult situations doesn't heal them. You leave everything behind to come to find you again. Look at Nate. What made you think that leaving was going to make your mom forget? You're not going to be able to stay away forever," Miller says.

"Putting all that aside," Max says leaning forward. "You were willing to throw away everything that we had without a word to us."

I shake my head, hating the edge there is to his voice. "It wasn't easy," I say. "I thought I was doing the best thing for everyone."

"You didn't give us a chance to tell you what we want," Mason says.

"You didn't give us a chance to be there for you," Max says.

"I thought you wouldn't want the hassle," I say, my throat burning as I realize just how much Nate's actions have affected the way I think about my worth.

"We care about you," Mason says. "More than should be possible after such a short amount of time."

Max puts his big hand over his heart. "You're here, Natalie," he says. "And you were willing to leave all this behind."

A tear escapes from my eye, and I swipe it away. "I didn't want to," I say, sounding choked. "I…I just don't even know how to deal with my feelings, the repercussions…none of it."

Mason stands, followed by his brothers. They crowd around me, laying their hands on my shoulders, wiping away my tears and smoothing my hair back from my face. I can't look into their eyes because I feel ashamed. Mason tips my chin and forces me to look up at him. "I get why all of this is too much for you. It's come too quick after you finished with that douchebag, and the family connection makes it complicated. But I want to know how you feel about us…put everything else aside and be honest."

I blink, the warmth I feel for them too much for me to contain anymore. My hand finds Mason's cheek, and he closes his eyes. My other hand seeks out Max and then Miller in the same way. Time slows as the connection between us swirls around me like a sun-warmed ocean. I want to give in to the pull. I want to feel their hands on me, their lips against my skin. I want to be surrounded by their strong bodies. I want to bask in the light of their smiles. I want to surrender to everything that should be wrong for me but feels too right to ignore.

When Mason's lips find mine, all the barriers that there were to us being together drop away. I don't have to do this alone. The decisions we make aren't all on me, despite what my mom said. Standing between them, I see that we're a unit. There might be four of us, but what affects one of us affects us all. Can I accept this enough to let go? Can I trust them enough?

All I know is how they make me feel. Secure and loved. Respected and admired.

I know how much they value me because they've gone out of their way to find me and put things right. They also pulled strings to help me find my dream job.

The job.

I pull back from Mason, my heart beating like a drum. "I took the job," I say. "I'm going to be leaving in two weeks."

They all grin, and I'm confused. Are they happy I'm leaving?

"That's amazing," Mason says.

"We knew you'd be perfect for the role," Miller says.

"Where will you be going to first?" Max asks.

"I'll be leaving. I'll be going overseas," I say, not sure they're really getting it. We have two weeks to enjoy together, and then it'll be over.

"We know," Mason says. "But we can visit you wherever you are."

"Any excuse for a luxury holiday," Miller laughs.

"And you'll be done in twelve months," Max smooths my hair. "A year will go past quickly. And phone sex can be really amazing. Think about all that building sexual tension."

"You don't mind?"

They shake their heads. "You have to live out your dreams, Natalie. This thing between us isn't about stifling any of us individually. It's about growing together." Miller always has a way of putting things, that immediately makes me feel better.

"It's like what you did for Mason…the gallery. He's going to be working from New York for a while now, but we can handle it. There'll be a time where we'll all come together…a time to create a home and start a family, but right now, our journeys can meander…it's time to spread our wings and learn to fly together." Miller and Mason turn to their brother with eyebrows raised. I guess Max isn't known for his profound outbursts, and I guess that just makes what he's said even more special.

"Seriously? You don't mind?"

They shake their heads. "Long distance will give us time to get to know each other even better."

"And I'm already imagining the reunion sex," Max smiles.

"Can we have some reunion sex now?" Miller asks.

"I'm thinking that Connie won't appreciate finding us in a tangle on her living room floor," I laugh. "But, there's a great hotel..."

Mason and Miller exchange grins. "Hotels are awesome," they say in unison.

"I'll book a room," Max says, already pulling his phone from his pocket.

My knees feel weak at the thought of what is going to come next.

Surrender to these three amazing men. Surrender to my heart and everything it craves.

And best of all, none of it at the expense of my dreams.

# 29

The air is humid enough to make my hair frizz and sweat trickle between my shoulder blades. I have my camera set on a tripod on the edge of one of the most beautiful mangrove areas I've ever seen. Coastal mangroves are among the most threatened ecosystems on earth, with current estimates indicating over two-thirds of mangroves have been lost to date. In Thailand, the pressure of economic expansion has resulted in the widespread loss of this valuable coastal habitat.

Knowing that the images I'm about to take will help to highlight the beauty and importance of something so under threat fills me with pride.

I know the light is optimal right about now. I take a look around, fascinated by the winding network of exposed roots, and the idea that these lush trees can live in saltwater. A crab scuttles, and I catch its funny sideways walk in the corner of my eye. In the distance, I hear what I think to be the call of a monkey.

I swipe at the beads of sweat developing at my hairline and forage in my side-slung canvas bag for some cool water.

My test shots are so close to perfect that I laugh out loud with satisfaction. The crab moves into the shot, and I can't believe my luck. The trees of the mangrove are hauntingly beautiful in their own right but the addition of the wildlife the mangrove sustains makes the shots that much more impactful. If I could catch the crab and kiss it for appearing at just the right moment, I would.

The second round of shots, including my new crustacean best friend are amazing. Henry, my colleague on this trip, will be so excited, and the crew back in the U.S. will have an easy time making these images tell the story of an endangered habitat that must be protected at all costs.

I watch the crab for as long as it's in view, stepping over roots to get close enough to make eye contact. He's a fiddler crab with one huge claw that makes it look as though he might tumble over as he rushes over the muddy floor of the mangrove. I know it's a he because of the oversized claw. "Hello," I say, then look around to make sure there is no one else in earshot. The local liaisons for our trip don't always understand our ways, and talking to crabs is likely to send rumors about my questionable sanity spreading amongst the group.

Eventually, my little buddy disappears into a muddy burrow, and I wipe my damp palms against my linen Thai fisherman's pants. They're so comfortable to wear that I've left most of my regular pants in my suitcase this trip, and they're so cheap too.

As I pack up my equipment, I start to imagine the cool water of the shower I will take when I return to my hotel.

It takes a very bumpy thirty-minute drive to get back to the small town we are staying in. I try to call Max on the journey, but he doesn't pick up. I miss my boys so much, especially when the distraction of my work is done. Those hours of alone time in the evening and early morning are when my heart aches and my body yearns. Phone sex can take the edge off the physical need, but I crave their touch in so many ways. I stare out of the window, remembering the last time we were all together. After the night at the hotel that turned into a three-day reunion that resulted in the stickiest, most tangled sheets I've ever had the pleasure of being partly responsible for, we had eleven more days of relishing each other and preparing for the changes that were heading our way.

At the airport, I'd tried to keep my composure but failed completely. I left my men with shirts wet with my tears. By the time I boarded the plane, my eyes were so puffy I could barely make out the row numbers to find my correct seat. The suited businessman sitting next to me was sensible enough not to try to make polite conversation. I sniffled into tissues for the lengthy flight, wondering if I'd made the right decision.

I know I have.

The last few months have been amazing. Awe-inspiring. The fulfilment of so many of my dreams.

And I've gotten to know my stepbrothers slowly. Miller was right. The long distance did give us time to learn slowly all the things that cement a relationship. Absence really has made the heart grow fonder. I can't wait to see them, although we still haven't managed to find a time when we can all meet.

My driver pulls into the impressive driveway at the front of the ornate hotel I am staying in. I gather my bags and throw the door open, struggling to pull my heavy camera bag with me as I leave the vehicle.

"Can I help you with that, ma'am?" a low deep voice says behind me. I stiffen, the familiarity of the voice making my heart speed. It sounds like Max but it can't be. Maybe I've missed them all so much that I'm starting to hallucinate! I turn slowly, the very idea that he could be so close too amazing to want to ruin immediately. Then I lay my eyes on Max and start to squeal because behind him are Mason and Miller, looking very pleased with themselves.

"Surprise," Mason says as I lower my bags to the ground and fling myself at them.

I can't form words I'm so overwhelmed, instead I hug them and inhale their scents that I missed so much. I grab big handfuls of their strong shoulders, and strong arms. I kiss their lips, holding their faces between my palms, not wanting to let them go for even a second.

"You're here," I say, when all the kissing and hugging has stolen my breath.

"We're here," Miller says with a grin.

"You should have told me. I would have organized a room upgrade."

"And miss all this?" Mason smiles with his dimples out in full force, looking so much like he did during the photoshoot that started everything.

"We've booked the honeymoon suite," Max says, his hand finding my ass and giving it a suggestive squeeze.

"Really. Have you?"

They nod, and we stand for a moment, gazing at each other, familiarizing ourselves with the real-life versions. They're taller than I remembered, and broader. Big. It's the word that fills my mind when I look at them. And handsome. So handsome.

"Let me get that," Max says, lifting my bags.

"And we'll show you the way."

"I'll need to get my things," I say.

"Later." Miller's voice is so firm that I heat between my legs. If there was ever an indication that he missed me, that one barked word is it!

"Okay," I say. "Take me to your lair."

They laugh, but Miller is a literal guy and suddenly I'm swept off my feet and lifted against his chest. I swat him with my hand, blushing as a couple waiting outside the hotel smiles in our direction. "I can walk," I say.

"But this is so much more fun!" he laughs.

The hotel staff all smile as we stroll through reception to the elevators. There are some quizzical looks but I don't care. I'm too happy to worry about what other people think. This is my life and I'm going to do everything I can to live it in a way that's going to make me happy.

At the door, Mason swipes the keycard. As we enter the room, I'm taken back to the day I got to Conrad's beach house and saw the view for the first time. The honeymoon suite has floor to ceiling windows overlooking the sea.

I don't get to spend any time gazing at it, though.

Miller has me on my back in seconds. "Tell me what you want," he orders.

"Everything," I gasp.

"Everything?" He raises is eyebrows and I nod. There are things we've been talking about over the phone that make my cheeks burn. Explicit things that I never wanted before. With Nate the idea made my skin crawl, but Nate is so far gone he might as well be dust. Everything is different now, including my hard limits.

"Everything," I say.

"Fuck," Max mutters. He knows what that means, taking no time to drop his shorts and boxers, fisting his decorated cock like a weapon. And it will be. A weapon of pleasure. I'm practically salivating.

Mason climbs onto the bed next to me. "So you don't want it soft and slow?"

"It's been too long," I say. "Make me feel it."

Mason's thumb slides over my lips, pushing inside my mouth. "This is where I'll go. I'd fit in here nicely."

"Is that what you want, Natalie? You want us to stuff you full?" I nod, gazing into Max's mesmerizing blue eyes, sucking on Mason's thumb while I feel Miller's hand edging between my legs. He touches my taint, the sensation as arousing as it is disconcerting.

"This is mine." His voice is so husky and low, I practically feel the vibrations against my clit. Mason pulls his thumb from my mouth so I can answer.

"Yours," I say softly.

"I'm going to lick you there first," Miller says. "You could come that way."

"I could?"

"Yeah. Then I'll open you gently with my fingers until you're stretched wide enough to take my cock."

"If that's what you want."

"Is it what you want?" Miller presses against my taint again and I feel a rush of heat over my clit. He has me panting, and I'm still fully clothed.

"Yes," I gasp.

"Fuck," Mason mutters.

"I need to freshen up first, though. I have mangrove mud on me."

The boys grumble but I promise I'll be quick. In the shower, I clean myself as thoroughly as I can, wanting everything about our time together to be perfect, but also needing to psych myself up. It's been months since I was with my stepbrothers face to face and that brings an unfamiliarity that I'm just not used to. I tell myself they're the same men they were when we were back in the US and the same men who've been there for me over the phone.

I smooth fragrant smelling lotion over my skin, relishing the curves I've developed over the past few months. Gone are the jutting hipbones that Nate pressured me to maintain. I have a womanly figure that I know my stepbrothers will love. I contemplate emerging in a towel, but that would be the old me. I don't want to be a person who hides again.

As I open the door, naked as the day I was born, I find my men lounging on the giant oversized bed. They're naked too and it almost knocks the breath from my lungs. They're perfection, outside and in. Three gorgeous men with huge hearts who've protected me fiercely. They think I don't know about what they did to Nate. Let's just say he won't be tempted to come near me again. It's a big relief.

I walk toward them with nothing but anticipation in my thoughts. When I climb on the bed, it's Max I straddle first. You'd think that would be an issue but jealousy isn't something that exists between my boys. They know I love them all with the same ferocity. They know they'll all get to have their fun and experience their pleasures. No rush. No competition. Just love.

I slide my pussy along the rigid bar of Max's cock, my already swollen clit taking all the delicious stimulation. I'm wet enough to fuck already which is a new phenomenon. As I lean down to kiss him, the bed shifts behind me and Miller does exactly what he promised he'd do. As his tongue laps at my clit, and then over my entrance and higher to my taint, I moan against Max's lips. Fingers find my nipples, pinching with just the right pressure. I take Mason's impressive cock in my hand, sliding up and down the rigid bar that's hot as hell and smooth as velvet. I know what he wants me to do with it, but he'll have to wait just a little.

The circling of Miller's tongue does exactly what he promised. My clit is pulsing, straining for contact. Inside, my pussy is fluttering with anticipation. Lick. Lick. Oh…I don't know how much more I can take. His fingers grip my hips, pressing into my flesh in a way they never could have before. I feel wanton and ripe, voluptuous and womanly. I feel worthy of their worship and that makes my chest ache in the best possible way.

"Don't stop," I say, but this time I don't get to decide.

Miller sucks on his fingers and eases them slowly back and forth where he'd been licking. Max takes his cock in hand, running the pierced head across my entrance, notching there but not pushing inside as Miller's thumb presses against my taint. There's a synchronicity about their actions, as though they know exactly what to do to make this easier and smoother for me.

The first press of Miller's thumb inside me has me bearing down on Max's cock and oh the stretch is too perfect. How did I go so long without this? How did my body cope without the intrusion of theirs?

"That's it," Miller says softly, moving back and forth, adding another digit, making me grunt. Max tugs my hips pulling me lower onto his cock until I feel the ache in my belly. He eases me down until I'm lying against his tattooed chest. Long strokes of his hot palm over my back joined by Mason's, calm me as Miller does what he needs to do to ready my body.

There are three men in my life. I want to know what it feels like to be totally possessed by them.

I hear a squeeze of a bottle, and cool liquid running between the cheeks of my ass. When Miller withdraws his fingers, I feel strangely empty, but when the blunt head of his big cock presses where his fingers were, I know the meaning of fullness.

"Just breathe," Max whispers.

"You've got this," Mason says softly.

"Fuck," Miller grunts as I begin to stretch to accommodate him. Oh it feels so good. The best kind of overwhelming. My heart pounds so loud in my ears it's like a drum punctuating a huge transition. This is me. I do what I like. I take what I want. I give pleasure without worry because the men who have my heart are good and generous and deserve everything in the world.

"She's so tight," Miller says.

"She's so full." Max tips my chin so I'm looking into his sexy eyes. "Are you okay? Does it feel good?"

"Better than good," I say as Miller draws back just a little, making my eyes roll.

It's so much. So amazing, but there is one thing missing.

Mason.

It takes all my concentration not to sink into the pleasure of the double penetration I'm experiencing because I need to push up onto my hands. I turn my head to where Mason is fisting his cock, his eyes fixed where his brothers are fucking into me. "I want to suck you," I say.

There's no hesitation. This is what we've talked about so much. The ultimate fantasy. Being filled by my three big men. I taste his arousal – salty sweet – as he pushes his cock into my mouth. It's a stretch to open my jaw wide enough, just like it's a stretch everywhere they're penetrating me, but I can take it. Gone is the timid Natalie who was always waiting for permission. Every thrust is an awakening of my future. These men have travelled around the world for me. They've given me back pieces of myself that I didn't even know I'd lost.

As Miller and Max thrust slowly, the piercing in Max's cock nudging the bundle of nerves inside me that I know has the potential to make me squeal, I do my best to give Mason all the pleasure he deserves. My vision clouds as my eyes leak tears. My pussy is so wet that the slick noises of Max's thrusts are loud and raw. But it's Miller who's working the hardest. I know how tough it must be for him to keep the slow and steady pace I need to stay comfortable. His hands are shaking against my hips as he fights to stay in control. Too fast and hard and he'll hurt me and that isn't what this is about.

I'm losing my battle to stay present, the graze of my clit against Max's body sending rushes of pleasure through me. I close my eyes, needing to focus because the orgasm that's building feels like something bigger than I've ever had to deal with.

A tsunami of pleasure forged by three men who own my body as much as they own my mind and heart.

My fingers grab handfuls of the clean white cotton sheets, grasping whatever it will take to anchor me. I groan around Mason's cock as my pussy clamps down and I shudder, my legs trembling with every pulse of pleasure.

"Fuck," Miller growls, moving even slower as I bear down around his cock in pulsating waves that are nothing I've ever felt before. This orgasm is all consuming. Violent. An exorcism of pleasure that is wringing me out. Mason comes first, spilling into my mouth in hot waves.

Max is next, his jaw clenched and head tipped back as he fights to deal with his orgasm as much as me. Miller is last, jerking in my most private of places, gripping my hips so hard I'll have bruises tomorrow.

Marks of ecstasy that I'll be proud to carry.

I don't remember how we end up lying together after. I'm sore everywhere, and swollen too. I press my hand between my legs, finding my clit bigger than it has ever been; teased to the point of oblivion. My body is wrung out but my heart is big.

"That was…" Miller says.

"Fucking amazing," Max finishes for his overwhelmed brother.

Mason kisses my lips. "Perfect," he says with a smile.

"I love you," I tell them. It's the first time I've said it but it feels so right, welling up from a heart that used to be fractured but is now whole.

"We love you too, Natalie," Max says stroking my hair.

Mason's fingers lace with mine and Miller's rests his hand on my shoulder. "This is everything we wanted. Everything we hoped for but didn't believe we could find."

For me it's more than I ever wanted. More than I could have ever believed I would have.

We rest together, drifting into sleep, and for the first time in a long time I feel peace.

I'm living my dreams and I haven't had to compromise for love. Instead, my amazing stepbrothers have set me on the path to true happiness. I know they'll always hold my heart with care and help me see a bigger and better me. We'll grow together; my stepbrothers and me.

# EPILOGUE

## TWO YEARS LATER

The room is quiet, which is precisely how I want it. I'm sitting on the bed, sliding on the thin gold sandals that I purchased for today. They're delicate and elegant while still being comfortable and practical for walking on the beach.

I stand, moving to take a final look at myself in the long mirror by the door, smiling at my reflection. The long, champagne-colored lace dress that I picked out is absolutely perfect, and the simple diamond-studded clip holding back just one side of my long hair brings just enough glamour to my appearance.

It might not be the kind of wedding dress that my mom imagined I would wear, but this isn't going to be the kind of wedding she imagined either. At least she's agreed to come and persuaded Conrad too. It means a lot to me and the triplets that our parents have finally accepted our relationship.

It hasn't been easy. They're old fashioned, I suppose, and they had different dreams for us all. Conrad had to let go of his sons all over again, and Mom simply didn't believe that I knew my mind enough to make such a decision. When I finally told her what happened with Nate, she thought I was acting on the rebound. Only time and perseverance has broken through all their negative perceptions.

The balcony door is open, and I still have ten minutes to spare, so I take a seat outside, inhaling the warm summer air and watching the waves break on the shore. The sand is so white here that it's almost blinding to look at. There was a time when I sat on a similar balcony in Thailand feeling as though my life was over. Nate had broken my heart, and I knew that I was coming to the end of a chapter in my life. A chapter I believed would be longer and more significant. I wept tears for all the paragraphs in my story that would never be written, finding the dreams that I'd woven slipping through my fingers, irretrievable. I made a vow that I wouldn't risk my heart again.

Then I met three men who showed me what it is to trust. They proved to me that I could listen to my internal voice and find a way to take control of my destiny. They made me realize that love doesn't have to be about sacrificing and standing still. It can be about growing and changing, finding fulfillment in our separate lives, and the parts of our lives that link us to others.

The past two years have been ones of discovery for us all. Mason has become one of the most sought-after new artists and is now painting full time, although he still lets me take the odd photo of him, just for fun and personal enjoyment! Miller took some time out from his practice and wrote a book on facing fears which hit the bestseller lists, and Max decided it was time to set up his own security company and now has contracts with several VIPs. He's still discreet about his clients, and although my nosy self would love to hear some gossip and scandal, I love that part of him too much to be disappointed.

When my year of taking photos for Eco-soldier had finished, I decided to set up a studio at home. It has meant that I can spend time with my men and still indulge in my passion for photography. I also have an annual two-month contract to refresh photography for three eco charities, which gives me a chance to travel and capture the landscapes that I'm so passionate about. It's a perfect balance. Mason has encouraged me to exhibit some of my personal shots, and I've begun to build a name for myself that way too.

I adjust the engagement ring that sits on my finger. It's a stunning three-stone diamond and platinum ring that my stepbrothers presented me with on our last holiday—three stones to represent the three most important men in my life.

Currently.

I rest my hand over my belly. There's a secret that I haven't shared with my stepbrothers yet. I've been saving the news until tonight.

There's a knock at the door, and I rise to answer, finding a very flushed Connie waiting to come in.

"Oh my god. You look…you look perfect," she gushes. "Just perfectly you."

"That was the aim," I smile. "And so do you." Connie is wearing a baby-blue strapless floor-length dress that fits with the wedding theme. She's my maid of honor, a special person to me who's been there for the ups and downs. A rock in both the calm and choppy waters of life.

"Did everyone arrive?" she asks.

"Yes. The flight got here a few hours ago." Conrad's brother's family was all delayed, so I was relieved when Miller called to let me know.

"And are you ready to go down?"

"Yes. Here…" I pass her the small bouquet of pretty white flowers that she'll be carrying, and reach for my slightly larger bouquet. I have my phone, room key, and lipstick in a small purse, which Connie will keep with her.

"Nervous?"

"I've never been calmer in my life."

She smiles, giving my arm a squeeze. "I'd hug you, but I don't want to mess this up." She waves her hand over me. "These boys really are the best."

"They are."

"But so are you, honey. You finally found not one but three men who deserve you. I'd say that's a pretty special feat."

"Well, if it wasn't for you, none of us would be here."

"I don't believe that. It might have taken you longer, but there is no way you would have resisted each other. All those family occasions. All that pent up sexual frustration."

"Yeah. I definitely wouldn't have been able to resist them, but it would have been different." As the saying goes, one door closes, and another opens. But everything in life is determined by the infinitesimal decisions made by each of us every second. That we ever achieve happiness and contentment sometimes feels like a miracle.

Connie holds the door open for me, and I pass through, feeling the importance of each step I take because they take me closer to my men. Closer to finding out the secret they've been keeping too.

The lobby is filled with beautiful floral decorations that are quintessentially Asian. The staff behind the reception smile happily, whispering to each other as we pass. The ceremony is taking place on the private beach in front of the ocean that always fills me with so much peace. I wish there were a way that I could legally marry all three of my men, but that kind of societal progress hasn't been made yet. I will promise myself to all of them, but only one will be my official husband.

They've kept who that will be from me. I don't know how they reached the decision, and I hope that the other two aren't disappointed. It will make no difference to me. There has never been any preferential treatment and there never will be. It's purely practical to ensure our children bear the Banbury name and that one of them is legally my next of kin.

It takes us a while to reach the beach, and Connie chatters about how much she's loved being in Thailand. It's her first trip overseas, so some of the enthusiasm comes from everything being a new experience, but it really is amazing here – the food, the culture, and the picturesque landscapes that never cease to steal the breath from my lungs.

Once we're close to the sea, I take a deep breath. There will never be a time that I'll live far from the ocean. The smell of it, the noise of the waves lapping calmly at the shore, they're the punctuation to my life.

And in front of me, standing beneath a beautifully decorated wedding arch, are my three stepbrothers. The harpist begins to play, and everyone turns to where Connie and I stand together. I smile broadly as I see that it's Max who's standing to the left. It's Max who'll take the vows for all of his brothers.

The walk down the sandy aisle between all our friends and family is overwhelming because this is all for us. Everyone is here to see us seal our love. At the front, I take in the sun-kissed faces of my husbands-to-be. In their linen suits, they look more handsome than I've ever seen them.

Max nods once - a check that I'm happy to proceed - and I beam to show him how happy I am. I would have felt the same no matter who was next to me.

The ceremony is quick and simple. There's no need to linger over something that feels so right. The vows I've written tell them of the difference they've made to my life and all of my hopes for our future. I'll always remember the way they look at me in the moment I promise myself to them for all of my life. They each reciprocate with words filled with so much love that Connie has to pass me a tissue.

When Max slides the wedding band onto my finger, I'm surprised to see it's Russian style ring with three intertwining bands of platinum, one for each of my men. Max and I make the formal promises, and he's the first to kiss my lips as a seal of our union, closely followed by both of his brothers. It's times like this that I wish I had another hand so that I could touch them all at the same time.

The congregation claps and cheers, and we turn to hug our parents. "All the happiness, my darling," Mom says, holding me close.

"I'm glad someone has finally taken them off my hands," Conrad jokes.

We've chosen to have our reception in the outdoor restaurant, serving a mixture of Thai and American food. I have a first dance with each of my husbands to a song chosen by them. Held close, I feel so safe in their arms.

Later, when Connie and I head to the bathroom to powder our noses she can barely contain her excitement. "The Banbury family are blessed with some great genes," she gushes.

"I know," I say. "I just married three of them!" Then I realize that she probably isn't referring to Mason, Miller and Max. I raise my eyebrows with interest. "Who's caught your eye?"

"Err…the twins."

"Who? Kane and Karter?"

"And Holden and Harris!"

"Mmmm…" Connie is right. There is definitely something magical in the DNA of my stepbrother's family.

"Well, I'm not sure what to tell you. I have no idea if any of them are single."

"They're probably all taken by tall, leggy blondes who spend all their time on Insta."

"You are gorgeous and any of them would be lucky to have you."

Connie smirks. "You're starting to sound like me."

"And you're starting to sound like me," I laugh. "Seriously, don't go there with the confidence issues. You'd eat those men up whole and spit them out and you know it."

Connie chuckles darkly under her breath. "Yeah, you're probably right. Anyway, no point in thinking about it. We're only here for a few more days and then it's back to real life."

"Well, a holiday fling could be very interesting. I can ask Mason about them? See if they have a thing for the reverse harem lifestyle."

"Maybe you could mention it." Connie wiggles her eyebrows and I splutter with laughter. "I didn't get a Brazilian wax so it could hide behind my swimsuit."

"Err…TMI," I giggle and then I decide that it's time to pull my bestie into a huge hug. She's been so instrumental in me arriving here in this happy place. It would be my absolute pleasure to help her find her feet too. "Love you, sweetie," I say.

"Love you too, Nat."

We emerge from our bonding session to find everyone on the dancefloor. The evening whizzes by and I have more fun than I've ever had before.

And later, when my stepbrothers lead me to our honeymoon suite, I'm completely ready for whatever path life will point us down. Big changes are coming, but will my stepbrothers be ready?

I don't remove my dress straight away. I tell them I want to sit on the balcony and breath in the sea air.

"This was the best day," Mason says.

"That's for sure," Max says, rolling up his sleeves, showing off his strong forearms and the tattoos that I've come to love.

"There will never be another like it," Miller says. He pops open a bottle of champagne and begins pouring us each a glass. I guess this is the perfect opening to tell them my secret.

"I can't drink that," I say as Miller hands me a glass.

"Why not? Do you have a headache?"

I shake my head, unable to stop the excited smile from pulling at my lips.

Miller narrows his eyes, and I can see his mind whirring. "Are you…?" He doesn't say the word, but I know he's worked it out.

"Yes," I say softly.

"What?" Mason and Max shout. "What's going on?"

Miller gazes at me with wide eyes that speak of wonder. I rest my hand over my slightly rounded belly, the babies nestled inside finally feeling real now their daddies know of their existence. Max drops to his knees, placing his hands next to mine. "You're having our baby?" he asks hopefully.

I nod. "Not just one, though," I say. "It's twins."

Mason laughs out loud in a sharp burst of delight. "Twins," he says as though he can't quite believe it's real.

"Twins," I say happily.

It's been hard to keep my pregnancy a secret, but I knew that revealing it on our wedding night was the best gift I could give my wonderful husbands.

"There's something else," I say after they've pulled me into hugs peppered with overwhelmed kisses that tell me exactly how happy they feel at the prospect of being fathers.

"What else?" Miller says with raised eyebrows.

I grasp my dress and pull it up gradually until my garter is revealed. Max whistles, thinking I'm ready to move on to wedding night fun. I will be soon, but not yet. Tugging the dress higher, I reveal my hip and the tattoo that I commissioned two weeks before; a heart with four birds in flight; A symbol of our relationship marked on my body forever. The heart is ours, finally whole and filled with love. The birds are me and my lovers, flying with the freedom we've blessed each other with to follow our dreams.

Max asks me to explain, using his index finger to trace the design as I do. I knew he'd be the one to understand and appreciate this the most because it's the way he marked his steps to freedom too.

"It's beautiful," he says. "Maybe you could add smaller birds to signify our children."

His sweet idea makes me smile.

As Mason takes my hand and leads me to our bedroom, I marvel at how far we've all come.

Even when the days seem dark, hope for a better future should always be in our minds. Maybe it's easy for me to say because everything worked out for me in the end. Maybe that's the best kind of perspective.

This thing between us was never supposed to be anything more than me getting myself back after a terrible relationship. It was supposed to be about mutual satisfaction and fun and freedom. And it has been about all of those things and so much more because that's where true love is forged.

# ABOUT THE AUTHOR

Stephanie Brother writes scintillating stories with bad boys and step-siblings as their main romantic focus. She's always been curious about the forbidden, and this is her way of exploring such complex relationships that threaten to keep her couples apart. As she writes her way to her dream job, Ms. Brother hopes that her readers will enjoy the full emotional and romantic experience as much as she's enjoyed writing them.

Printed in Great Britain
by Amazon